RAVEN
AVENGING

JERRY RICE

BEAVER'S POND
PRESS

Edited by Wendy Weckwerth

ISBN 13: 978-1-59298-830-3
Library of Congress Catalog Number: 2017902373
Printed in the United States of America
First Printing: 2017
21 20 19 18 17   5 4 3 2 1

Book design by Athena Currier

Beaver's Pond Press, Inc.
7108 Ohms Lane
Edina, MN 55439–2129

(952) 829-8818
www.BeaversPondPress.com

To order, visit www.ItascaBooks.com or call
1-800-901-3480 ext. 118. Reseller discounts available.

For more information, visit JerryRiceRavenAvenging.com.

This book is dedicated to the victims of human trafficking and to the defeat and damnation of all procurers and pimps worldwide.

But, above all, it is dedicated to Pat, the love of my life.

Then shall ye do unto him, as he had thought to have done unto his brother: so shalt thou put the evil away from among you. And those which remain shall hear, and fear, and shall henceforth commit no more any such evil among you. And thine eye shall not pity; but life shall go for life, eye for eye, tooth for tooth, hand for hand, foot for foot. When thou goest out to battle against thine enemies, and seest horses, and chariots, and a people more than thou, be not afraid of them; for the Lord thy God is with thee, which brought thee up and out of the land of Egypt.

—Deuteronomy 19:19–21; 20:1

We have heard from the South how Gunnar, Warrior of many seas,
Passionate in battle,
Wielded his mighty halberd.
Waves of foreman broke
On the cliffs of his defense

—Njal's Saga

PROLOGUE

September 1976

I T WAS A BALMY SEPTEMBER NIGHT in Times Square, and the streets teemed with frenetic activity. Hustlers, junkies, and hookers mingled with crowds of theatergoers, young servicemen on leave, sightseers, and seekers of sex, drugs, and adventure. A cab pulled up to the curb in front of one of the shabby, redbrick hotels in the low forties, just off Times Square, dropping off two young sailors. As the sailors paid their fare amid calls from the small throng of prostitutes lounging around the awning in front of the hotel, a young, blonde hooker, ponytail streaming behind her, dashed out of a doorway halfway down the block. Carrying her spike heels in both hands, she sprinted for the cab, throwing herself inside just as the cabbie was resettling into his seat.

"Wait a minute," said the cabbie. "You got cash?"

Desperately fumbling in her purse, she found a crumpled twenty and handed it to him. Tears streamed down her cheeks as she implored him, "Move, please! *Drive!*"

1

A twinge of pity came over the cabbie, and he drove away from the curb. Watching the young whore in the rearview mirror, he saw her looking anxiously over her shoulder as the cab pulled down the street.

"Where to, lady?"

"Kennedy Airport, please."

As the cab reached the corner of Avenue of the Americas and headed down to Thirty-Sixth Street for the Queens-Midtown Tunnel, the cabbie asked. "Which airline?"

"Northwest."

Passing under the East River and emerging from the tunnel, the cabbie noticed some of the anxiety leave the face of the young woman. Nothing more was said all the way to the airport, but the cabbie speculated about whom she was running from and where she was going.

Finally, they pulled up in front of the Northwest Terminal. As she paid him, the cabbie gave her a smile. "Good luck, wherever you're going," he said.

She was surprised, unaccustomed to kindness. "Thanks. It's about time I had some luck."

As the cab pulled away, she turned toward the terminal, walking as rapidly as her spike heels would allow. A cream-colored van, back cargo doors standing open, stood at the curb. As the young woman passed, a burly man in coveralls stepped toward her and seized her arm. Pulling her toward him, he clasped a huge, hairy hand over her mouth and began dragging her into the van. The driver, also in coveralls, slammed the rear doors behind them. Several busy travelers saw what occurred, paused, and then averted their eyes and hurried to catch their flights. As the van pulled into traffic, the woman bit deeply into the hand of her captor and broke free. Powerful hands grasped one of her ankles as she lunged for the passenger door. Flailing with her fists and kicking with her free foot, she felt herself being pulled back to the floor by a strength far greater than her own. The battle continued in the back of the van as the driver wove in and out of traffic on the way back to Manhattan.

1

THE COYOTE FLOATED OVER THE GROUND like a small puff of gray peat smoke. Gunar "Raven" Ravendal marveled at how the animal adeptly used all available cover in the meadow as it worked its way ever closer to his brother's sheep. He waited until the coyote skylined himself on a small rise, just before his intended final rush down upon the flock. The sharp crack of his .300 Remington shattered the crystalline stillness of the morning. One hundred fifty yards away, the coyote, head shot, leaped high in the air, ran in a tight circle, and collapsed to the ground.

Whereas most riflemen wouldn't risk a head shot at such a distance, Raven always did when taking animals with valuable pelts. As he moved toward the dead predator, the sheep, scattered by the report of the rifle, began to return to the meadow. Raven approached the carcass, carefully set his rifle against the fence, took out his buck knife, and began skinning. He was pleased with the clean kill, which left the pelt in prime condition. Working with sure, deft strokes of the knife, within ten minutes he had removed the pelt. He left the carcass as a reminder to the coyotes and wolves that periodically slipped across the Canadian border to prey on Lorne's sheep.

Gunar and his older brother, Lorne, though close, looked about as different as two Minnesota brothers of Norse background could. Gunar took his nickname from his raven-black hair, the result of latent genes that proved Viking raids had extended into the Mediterranean. Only his size—six foot two and 210 pounds—and his striking gray eyes evidenced that centuries-past Viking heritage. The darkness of his skin, bronzed by a life in the woods, swamps, and fields, gave further credence to his nickname. Maybe it was the bestowing of the nickname by his father, Lars, thirty-five years earlier that motivated Raven to take to the wild country as he had. Perhaps he would have permanently migrated to his beloved Alaska or the Northwest Territories had Lars not toiled so mightily here, opening the homestead along the Canadian border and leaving it equally to his two sons.

Lorne, a more traditional northern Minnesotan, was an ideal complement to Raven in the farming operations. Whereas Raven, the restless one, was constantly experimenting with new crops and techniques in conjunction with his friends on the agronomy faculties of the Universities of Minnesota and North Dakota, Lorne took pride in perfecting a classic, diversified farming operation. The sheep were a good example. Raven disliked the steady husbandry connected with sheep, not to mention cattle and poultry, because they tended to restrict his travels to Alaska and the Northwest Territories. Blond, jovial Lorne often jokingly pointed out the times income from wool, eggs, and cream had spelled the difference between financial survival or being forced to sell off parts of their beloved homestead.

Raven took the ribbing with good humor, partly because it reminded him of Lars's teasing during his boyhood but also because he knew the considerable wealth of the two brothers flowed primarily from the gambles Raven had forced upon them—opening up peat lands to experimental varieties of domestic bluegrass, pioneering with sunflower cultivation in the area, and gambling on new, disease-resistant varieties of wheat, barley, and oats. On the other hand, he had to concede that Lorne's abhorrence of noxious weeds on the older lands was one of the key factors in the willingness of agronomists and seed companies to provide them with experimental varieties of seeds. And Lorne's love of machinery and his spotless, well-equipped machine shop had never failed to impress the bankers.

Raven's one great mechanical passion was the gunsmith shop he had inherited from Lars. Indeed, working with Lars there—loading shells and working stocks, barrels, and firing mechanisms during the long, dark winter evenings—had been the one thing that brought him close to his father. In all other respects, Lorne and Lars had been alike, not only in their penchant for teasing but also in their passion for the stewardship of the land.

While Raven had excelled in athletics and had gone away to college, Lorne could never tear himself away from the farm long enough to partake in any outside activities other than 4-H Club projects connected with the farm and winter courses at the agricultural college.

It was a surprise when vivacious, golden-haired Beverly Olson ended her long-standing flirtation with Raven and accepted Lorne's devoted courtship. Lorne was scarcely known in the area since his graduation from high school three years earlier, except in its agribusinesses and the small Lutheran church five miles from their farm in the northwestern corner of the county. Beverly's parents, pillars of the community, had looked askance at the courtship. Then one evening, Helmer Lee, president of Farmers and Drover's Bank, having imbibed considerably more than usual, violated one of his cardinal rules and spoke a bit too freely about the value of the Ravendal brothers' holdings. From that point on, with the subtle encouragement of Beverly's parents, the romance flourished, with long walks along the river, regular church attendance at the big Lutheran church in town, and quiet conversations about love of family, God, and country.

Even in his role as best man at the wedding, Raven managed to hide his feelings from everyone but Beverly. Turning from the traditional kiss at the altar, she spied the wild look of pain in the gray depths of his eyes and wondered what would become of the brothers' farming partnership.

For a time, it appeared Raven was gone from their lives forever. Word came back in midwinter that he was hunting and trapping in the Canadian wilderness and was living with a Cree woman. Toward spring, Lorne began to wonder aloud if Raven had "gone back to his people," as he jokingly put it.

In truth, he missed working out their spring planting charts together and longed for his return. By late April, Lorne was in a genuine quandary about what crops to seed on the new land Raven had opened up on the north end of their farm. Finally, he began wondering whether or not he should set out in search of his brother. He kept putting it off, dreading what he might hear if he pressed the issue.

One day, just before planting in mid-May, Raven returned, looking even more tanned and fit than ever.

"Tried to get lost in the woods," he said, grinning at Lorne. "Guess I've got a compass in my head, pointing back to this farm, because I didn't succeed." Both brothers were amazed to find themselves fighting back tears as they playfully punched one another on the shoulder and wrestled around in a circle to cover their emotions.

Beverly appeared in the doorway of their home and with a smile said, "You hid out in those woods so long you never had a chance to learn you're going to be an uncle!"

Raven's obvious joy at the news instantly knit the three of them together again. From that point on, the pathway through the aspen woods from the old, original homestead where Raven lived to the new home of Beverly and Lorne became well used. After the birth of Kari, it became even more well-worn as she grew into a tomboy dogging her uncle Raven's steps. She took a real interest in his conservation projects, learning of his decision to allow beaver dams to create ponds in the wooded areas, and his reintroduction of prairie chickens, bluebirds, and other species to his thriving, wild-grass prairie.

One day, they saw a great horned owl attack a raven's nest. After watching the furious aerial combat, which ended in the death of the mother raven, they walked to the base of the nest tree and found two raven chicks. Since the chicks couldn't survive in the wild, Raven and Kari took them home and raised them as pets. Kari nicknamed them Honey and Money, after Raven suggested she might name them after the Norse god Odin's pet ravens, Hugin and Munin.

When the chicks grew big enough to fly, Kari and Raven released them back to the wild. But they remained around the farm as delightful, mischievous, half-wild pets flying out to greet visitors, swooping down for offered treats, croaking out avian commentary, and stealing any shiny objects left lying about.

Raven continued to turn female heads whenever he visited the universities. With the exception of two short-lived, long-distance romances—one with a literature professor and another with an opera singer—he devoted all his energies to wildlife, farming, and Lorne, Beverly, and Kari. When Little Lars arrived four years later, it was obvious that he was cast out of the Lars-Lorne mold. It became a family joke that Little Lars was a permanent fixture on all of Lorne's equipment and in his pickup, because he never seemed to leave his father's side. Before long, he was mimicking his father's mannerisms perfectly.

The relationship of Little Lars and Lorne seemed to cause Raven and Kari to become even closer than before. On the morning of Kari's tenth birthday, Raven appeared at her bedroom door.

"Get dressed quickly, Kari," he said. "I've got a surprise for you."

As they hurried out the door, across the farmyard and through the aspens to Raven's place, Kari's eyes sparkled. "What is it, Uncle Gunar?" she kept asking, unable to contain herself.

"Wait and see," was all she could get out of him.

Then he led her into the barn. There, in the big box stall in the corner, was a beautiful, yearling Appaloosa filly, with a deep-gray coat, a white star on her forehead, and classic dappled-gray hindquarters.

"She's yours, Kari," Raven said, smiling. "We'll have to break and train her. I thought it might make a good 4-H project for you. Now you'll be able to ride on your own horse. You're getting too big for riding double with me all the time."

Kari was beside herself with excitement. "Oh, Uncle Gunar, I love her!" she exclaimed, throwing her arms around his neck.

Raven's eyes misted over as he returned the hug. Covering his emotions, he lifted her high above him and spun around and then gently set her down. "We'll have to be careful around her at first," he said. "After we get her gentled down, we can begin getting her used to a saddle, little by little. I'll show you how."

Over the months, as they trained and broke the Appaloosa, Raven and Kari grew even closer. They were an inseparable pair, working in the stable, training the little mare in the corral, and finally riding all over the farm and surrounding country. Kari turned into an accomplished rider. As her collection of ribbons and trophies grew, Raven was her number-one fan and constant companion. And their hell-for-leather riding around the farm, whooping and yelling through the fields, over fences, and through the farmyard was the joy of the entire family.

When Kari decided to move down to Minneapolis with some friends the summer after she graduated from high school, Raven was deeply shaken. "Your Appaloosa and I might miss you a little bit," he told her as she left. "You probably ought to look in on us once in a while."

"Oh, Uncle Raven, you know you'll always be my best boyfriend," she said, attempting to keep things light.

As he watched the carload of Minneapolis-bound girls pull away, he wondered if things would ever be the same again.

2

CARRYING THE FRESH COYOTE PELT IN ONE HAND, Raven decided to show it to Lorne and Little Lars before stretching it out to cure. As he left the wood-lot and entered Lorne's yard, he gave the old frontiersman's call that had become a family joke: "Halloo, the house. Hold your fire. I'm coming in!" To his surprise, neither Lars nor Lorne offered their usual, "Come on in!"

As he entered through the kitchen door, Raven's blood ran cold as he heard hacking sobs emerging from somewhere deep in his brother's broad chest. Beverly sat at the kitchen table, holding Lorne's hand, tears streaming down her face. Little Lars stood beside his father's chair with his face buried in Lorne's huge, heaving shoulder. Raven dropped the pelt, leaned his rifle in the corner of the porch, and sat down at the table. Beverly silently pushed a telegram to him.

TO LORNE RAVENDAL FAMILY STOP
PLEASE ADVISE AT ONCE STOP CAN
YOU PROCEED IMMEDIATELY TO
NEW YORK TO IDENTIFY BODY

OF APPROXIMATELY EIGHTEEN-
YEAR-OLD CAUCASIAN FEMALE
BELIEVED TO BE KARI RAVENDAL
STOP MATCHES MISSING-
PERSON DESCRIPTION GIVEN
BY MINNEAPOLIS ROOMMATE
TWO WEEKS AGO STOP CONTACT
LIEUTENANT WILLIAM MASSEY,
NYPD, 212-555-7613.

From then on, everything took on a surreal quality, like a nightmare interrupted with fitful awakenings only to begin again, horrible and unreal.

Raven scarcely remembered leaving Beverly and Little Lars with Beverly's parents and the long drive to Grand Forks with the silent and scarcely functioning Lorne beside him. Occasionally, during the flights to Chicago and New York, Raven pondered the callousness of the New York police, sending the news by telegram, without even a personal telephone call, let alone a visit by a pastor or other intermediary.

Upon their arrival at the office of Lieutenant Massey, it was apparent he regarded the death as nothing out of the ordinary in the life of a hardened Manhattan homicide detective. Lorne moved as if in a trance during the visit to the morgue.

The morgue visit was a nightmare for both Raven and Lorne. The gleaming stainless-steel table and white tile walls seemed garish and cruel. When the technician uncovered Kari's body, both brothers gasped at the sight of her bruised face, legs, and arms and the combined look of terror and fury on her face. Her bright-blue eyes were glazed and lifeless, a stark contrast to the liveliness that had been her greatest attribute the last time she was among her loving family.

Back at Massey's office, the veteran detective began explaining the situation to the bereaved father and uncle. "Once a young woman enters the life of a prostitute, her life expectancy drops dramatically. It's not unusual for us to be confronted with five of these deaths per month. These girls that come in via the 'Minnesota pipeline' are often broken in somewhere else, such as Chicago or Cleveland, and then sold into the New York trade. As you saw at the morgue, the victim had fresh needle tracks on her arms. There were also fairly recent cigarette burns and marks from beatings with a coat hanger. This all leads us to believe that the victim was recruited fairly recently in Minneapolis and offered some resistance, wherever she was broken in."

In the face of the lieutenant's dispassionate recital of the grim facts, Raven finally exploded. "Goddamn you, she is not 'the victim,' she's our Kari! Where we come from, mister, every one of us has a name! Every one of us counts! We don't forget!" he roared, taking a step forward.

Massey was unaccustomed to backing down from any apparent threat, but something in the thunderous rage in Raven's voice and the fire in the pale-gray eyes made him step back. "C'mon, now. Let's calm down. I'm terribly sorry. It's just that we see so much tragedy here and we deal with so much frustration . . ."

Lorne grabbed his brother's arm and murmured, "Please, Raven, this won't do any good. Let's take her home."

Together, the grief-stricken brothers filed out of Massey's office and made arrangements for Kari's transportation home.

3

ELMO "FLASH" MARUSKA HAD BEEN SUFFERING severe stomach cramps all morning. The experience was nothing new—it happened every time Rosalee and he embarked on another one of their diets. At breakfast that morning, Flash calculated that they had lost at least a ton, collectively, during their thirty-two years of marriage. Naturally, Flash—whose playing weight had been 265 the day he earned his nickname by tipping a pass, catching it, and rumbling fifty-five yards for a touchdown while packing three Rutgers players on his back—had lost the lion's share of the ton. Saucy Rosalee (née Petraglia), at five foot three inches and frequently spectacular proportions, had probably only accounted for three to four hundred pounds of losses in their dieting careers. The remainder of the losses were caused by Flash's gargantuan appetite and swings of weight, which had ranged from 275 to 350 and was distributed in interesting ways at various times over his six-foot-seven frame.

As a result, Flash had accumulated the largest wardrobe of any member of the United States Department of Justice's organized crime strike force for the entire Southern District of New York. The wardrobe reflected his various weights during his entire history of professional football, graduate school in criminology, various ranks with the NYPD, and now the organized crime strike force. The brute fact of the matter was that Rosalee and Flash's great passion in life was food in all forms, ranging from her ethnic Italian cookery to the gourmet French recipes she was constantly clipping from her many food magazines. So far, Rosalee had prepared numerous dishes that held no appeal for her, but she had yet to make a recipe that met with anything less than complete enthusiasm from Flash. Except for the diets. Flash couldn't believe he'd endured another breakfast of grapefruit, a hard-boiled egg, and black coffee.

So the appearance of Henry Grogan in his office brought genuine relief. Flash hoped it would take his mind off his grumbling stomach. Grogan and Flash had been a team ever since their rookie days at NYPD. A dedicated bachelor who endured teasing because of his uncanny resemblance to Colonel Potter of *M*A*S*H*, Grogan was a shrewd and detail-oriented complement to the inspired energy and intuition of his massive partner, Flash. His penchant for occasionally allowing himself a few extra Bushmills after work was a small price to pay for what he brought to the team.

"Got a new one for you, Flash," shot Grogan. "Rumor on the street is that Dom Cerrillo's kid, Vito, has decided to get himself a big string of hookers. The story is, he whacked three pimps in the Times Square area before five more decided it was reasonable to sell out and head back to Chicago or Cleveland or Detroit or wherever the hell they came from. Further, it seems a new hooker for one of the black dudes Vito whacked took the opportunity to try to run back to Minnesota, or wherever she came from. Seems Vito didn't like his recently acquired livestock running off, so he called Daddy Dom to alert his hijack crews and spotters at all the airports. Two of Dom's boys apparently grabbed her as she got out of a cab at Kennedy, but she put up such a fight on the way back to town that one of Vito's crew got excited and snuffed her."

"Cause of death?"

"Manual strangulation."

"We got anything that pins it to Dom or Vito?"

"Naw, you know how it is." Grogan sighed. "The only tie is Dom's pet mouthpiece. He posted bail and sprang the goon."

"Thanks, Henry. Probably won't help us much, but it gives us something new to watch."

Flash took his pen and wrote *prostitution* on a small card on his desk. Getting out of his chair, he towered over Grogan and the bulletin board behind him. On the portion of the bulletin board devoted to the Cerrillo family, under the category *Illegitimate Activity*, he added the prostitution card below *hijacking*, *labor racketeering*, *loan-sharking*, *extortion*, *bookmaking*, *numbers*, *narcotics*, *illegal tobacco*, and *tippling houses*. After a moment's reflection, he put a question mark after *prostitution* and then drew lines with question marks between *prostitution* and *narcotics* and then drew lines with question marks between *prostitution* and *narcotics* and *prostitution* and *tippling houses*. Next, after checking the validity of the report from Grogan's source (who Grogan refused to reveal), Flash called his old friend Charlie Howell at the FBI and reported Grogan's story. He then called Lieutenant William Massey at the NYPD with the same information. At the end of the call, Flash was surprised by Massey's reaction. "I wish to hell we could put little Vito in a room along with the victim's uncle. There was something about those folks that kinda got to me after they ID'd the body today. Sometimes I wish I wasn't hemmed in by the badge."

Flash Maruska paused for a few moments, staring at the list of the Cerrillo family's legitimate and illegitimate enterprises. Then his stomach began to rumble again. He reached into his desk and pulled out the pathetically tiny Tupperware container of chicken salad seasoned with vinegar and a tablespoon of diet mayonnaise.

"Whoopee." He sighed.

4

F UNERALS AT PINE KNOLL LUTHERAN always seemed to come on black, windy days. Raven sat next to Little Lars in the Ravendal family pew, listening to the wind as it whistled and howled along the white clapboard siding of the church. As Pastor Martinson earnestly tolled the liturgy of the funeral service, Raven kept himself from breaking down by concentrating on comforting Little Lars. By the time the soprano soloist completed the Norwegian funeral hymn "Behold a Host, Arrayed in White," tears were streaming down the faces of all the Ravendal relatives and friends who had packed the little church. Lars, Beverly, and Little Lars were close to complete despair during the trip through the grove to the cemetery. Raven fought for control at the graveside service. He was thankful when a September squall came, washing the tearstains from his face.

Then relatives and friends surrounded the family and accompanied them back to the fellowship hall in the church basement for a meal prepared by the Pine Knoll Lutheran Ladies Aid. The family seemed to be doing a little better as they accepted the condolences of their friends. Raven compartmentalized his grieving, not wishing to share it with anyone but Lorne, Little Lars, and Beverly.

During the period of fellowship, Carl Johnson, one of his favorite cousins from boyhood, came up to him. Carl's father had moved the family to California when Carl was ten but had sent Carl back to his grandpa's farm every summer. He and Raven were the same age and had enjoyed each other's company over five summers of haying, hunting, fishing, and baseball. Raven heard Carl had inherited his father's shipping business in Los Angeles and was prospering. He felt a glow of appreciation that Carl would travel all the way from California for the funeral. As Raven reached to shake hands with him, he was surprised when Carl extended his left hand rather than his right. He involuntarily glanced down at Carl's right hand.

Even bearing bad news, Carl couldn't stop smiling, it was so ingrained in his nature. "Raven, I know you have enough troubles right now. Maybe I'll have a chance to explain later. Let's just say I used a bank in LA I didn't know enough about, and now I have some new business partners I wish I'd never met. I didn't mind so much when they mangled my fingers in the car door. But when they started calling and telling me the kids' routes to and from school, I decided I'd better not fight. I'm sorry about Kari. Too bad our family has to learn about big-city ways the hard way, eh?"

Raven pondered Carl's words as he accepted the condolences of more family members and friends. Toward the end of the fellowship, Kari's friend Beth came up to him.

"Raven, I told Kari not to go with that guy. She said I was just prejudiced and afraid of blacks, and that we just didn't understand."

"What guy?"

"I don't know his real name. But the license plate on his big white Continental said *Junebug.*"

"How did she meet him?"

"He came up to us when we were leaving a movie down on Hennepin Avenue. He asked Kari if he could buy her a cup of coffee. She told him no, and then he asked her, 'What's wrong? Are you afraid to have a cup of coffee with a black man?' It seemed like Kari was trying to prove she wasn't prejudiced, so she had a cup of coffee with him, and he gave her a ride home in his Continental. Then he started sending her flowers and candy and stuff. It seemed like Kari was drifting away from us and into his circle. But she kept insisting he was such a gentleman. Just before she disappeared, he gave her this beautiful friendship ring."

"When she disappeared, why didn't you call Beverly and Lorne?"

"Well, Kari said Junebug had promised her a trip to Chicago, and we were afraid we might get her in trouble with her folks, you know. She left on Friday, so she didn't miss any work until she had been gone for two workdays. By Wednesday, we called the cops. They said they knew about Junebug and they'd try to run him down. The Minneapolis cop said Junebug's got a record a mile long with the Vice Squad. They know he's a pimp, but they said it's hard to catch pimps. If we'd known sooner, we would've told Kari . . . but she was gone." Beth's eyes welled up with tears, and she began shaking uncontrollably.

Raven tried to comfort Beth, taking her in his arms and patting her shoulder. But inside, a cold rage was building.

He somehow kept himself from breaking down for the rest of the evening at the church and all the way back to Beverly and Lorne's place. There was little he could do for his family except be with them. Eventually, exhausted, Beverly and Little Lars turned in. Lorne sat staring out the window until long after midnight. Finally, he let Raven give him some warm milk and aspirins to help him sleep, and he hauled himself to bed.

Scuds of clouds were racing by the moon as Raven walked through the woods and back into the clearing of his home. Out of habit, he turned into the stable to look after the horses. As usual, his big bay gelding was rattling his oats bucket, noisily demanding to be fed. Raven bent to fill the bucket for both the bay and Kari's Appaloosa. When he straightened, he felt the soft muzzle of the Appaloosa against his neck. It took him off guard, and he finally broke. Great, hacking sobs racked his body as he buried his head in the Appaloosa's neck. After a long time, the sobbing and the tears ceased. The Appaloosa seemed to sense that he'd found a measure of peace. Nickering softly, she left the stable to join the bay in the corral.

Raven slowly walked to the old log-cabin homestead his father had built. As he entered his den, his gaze fell on the gun rack, and the rage he'd felt at the church returned. He selected four weapons—his .270 Winchester bolt-action deer rifle, his new Ruger automatic 10/22 carbine, his Browning automatic 12-gauge shotgun, and his old Winchester Model 50 shotgun with the short skeet barrel. After carefully dismantling and cleaning all four, he returned the Browning and .270 to the rack. For the remainder of the night, Raven sat in the moonlight, carefully oiling and working the mechanism of the Model 50. Finally, as dawn broke, he nodded off to sleep.

The web is now woven
and the battlefield reddens;
the news of disaster
will spread through lands.
It is horrible now
to look around
as a blood red cloud
darkens the sky.
Heavens are stained
with the blood of men,
as the Valkyries
sing their song.
We sang well
victory songs
for the young king:
Hail to our singing!
Let him who listens
to our Valkyries' song
learn it well
and tell it to others.
Let us ride our horses
hard on bare backs,
with swords unsheathed
away from here.

—Njal's Saga

5

October 1976

JUNIOR "JUNEBUG" JOHNSON WAS FEELING MARVELOUS.
The evening had gone *so smooth*. Back to the Twin Cities
from that ugly hassle in the Big Apple, Junebug had
immediately returned to his old haunts. And after two days,
old Junebug's luck had held true again, this time in the form
of a splendiferous, young, brunette bitch from Iowa, fresh
off the farm. Junebug had met her in the bus terminal and
was happy to offer his services, helping the young lady to the
YWCA for her first night in the big city. On the way, like all
the others, in response to Junebug's sorrowful question, the
lady had righteously allowed as how she was not too prejudiced to have a cup of coffee with a black man.

Junebug sang softly as the Continental slid through the
night, "Ole Junebug, you got class, and it's class that gets the
ass. Ole Junebug's elegant threads leads 'em right to Junebug's
bed," he kept rhyming. He chuckled as he thought of how
the little brunette's eyes had bugged open tonight when he'd
slipped the gorgeous sapphire friendship ring on her finger

and how eager her lips had been as he chastely kissed her good-night.

"With the lungs on this bitch, ole Junebug's gonna be in clover again. Here's to the Minnesota Pipeline!" He laughed. As his Continental swung along Mississippi River Boulevard, Junebug turned up the stereo and rolled down the windows. The cool autumn air felt like a tonic as he opened the windows and took out his inhaler. A little cocaine rush would make the evening sheer ecstasy. Junebug didn't notice the mud-splattered black Ramcharger that had been following him all the way from the Iowa girl's new apartment that Junebug had helped finance. As the black vehicle pulled abreast of him on the deserted boulevard, Junebug finally glanced over. His eyes popped open in disbelief at what he saw. The business end of a 12-gauge pointed straight at his head! As he turned down the radio, he heard the shouted command, "Pull into the rest area!"

Sumbitch, Junebug thought. *Is this motherfucker some kind of goddamn ever-lovin' narc, or is he a new man on Vice?* As he got out of his Continental, it never dawned on him that he wasn't being righteously rousted. As both cars pulled into a parking lot on the bluffs, high above the Mississippi, Junebug held up his hands. "Hey, man, what's the beef? You don't need to pull no shotguns on ole Junebug." Then he noticed the look in the stranger's eyes. A chill ran up his spine. "Hey, man, y'all from downtown? What's with you, anyhow?"

"I've got something for you from Kari Ravendal."

Suddenly, something Kari had said clicked in Junebug's mind. "Hey, man, you wouldn't be great, big Uncle Raven, now would you? Bet y'all wouldn't be so goddamn tough without that shotgun," he said as he pointed. "Heard about your poor niece. Man, you barking up the wrong tree. If you got a beef, you oughta see Little Vito Cerrillo in the Big Apple. So why don't you get the hell outta my face!" he snarled. "Big fuckin' man with a big fuckin' shotgun."

To his amazement, he saw Raven put the shotgun on the fender of the Ramcharger and advance toward him. Junebug quickly pulled his straight razor from his sock. Raven wrapped his jacket around his left forearm and continued his advance.

As the two circled for advantage, Junebug commenced taunting again. "Fuckin' honky white bread, I'm gonna cut your gizzard out. And it's gonna pleasure me almost as much as branding your dear little niece and shooting her up pleasured me and my number-one lady!" he shouted as he lunged.

Suddenly, his razor hand was held in a steely grasp that exuded a power Junebug had never felt in another human being. His eyes opened in terror as he looked in Raven's wild, steel-gray eyes. Not those of a modern man but of a berserker Viking intent on revenge.

A thunderous right fist crashed into his breastbone, dropping Junebug to his knees. The razor clattered on the pavement. As his head snapped left and right and left and right again and again from the blows raining down on his face, Junebug began to lose consciousness. He dimly realized he was being lifted onto the hood of his Continental. His raw silk trousers were slashed open. He had a brief moment of consciousness as the razor-sharp buck knife expertly sliced off his testicles and penis and a fleeting recognition of the warm flow of his own blood down his legs. But by the time he'd been hauled back to the front seat of the Continental, his mouth pried open, and his cock and balls stuffed into it, Junebug had no more memories. What a rush it would have been if he could've watched as the Continental was doused with gasoline, rolled to the edge of the cliff, and set ablaze just before it careened two hundred feet down to the beach of Ole Man River!

The following morning, a cold drizzle was falling as Detective Sergeants Pearson and Givins, Minneapolis Police Department, surveyed the charred wreck of Junebug's car.

"Goddamn," said Pearson.

"Goddamn, that slimy motherfucker Junebug finally bought it," echoed Givins in a tone of disbelief.

"But what do you make of the way he bought it? I mean, up north where I come from, I heard once about the Red Lake Chippewa operating like that on a guy who raped an Indian gal. But stuffing his equipment into his mouth, setting fire to him, and running him off a cliff . . . goddamn. I heard about things like that in 'Nam, but never in Minnesota."

"Well," Givins offered, "maybe that's a lead. Maybe we're looking for a Chippewa brother who served in 'Nam."

"I don't know. I just don't know."

"So you think we oughta sort of let this slip out down on Hennepin?" mused Givins.

6

L ATE FALL FOUND RAVEN BACK AT THE FARM, helping
Lorne, Beverly, and Little Lars deal with their grief
and seeing to the storage and sale of their crops. This
year, instead of heading to Alaska for a winter of trapping,
Raven worked on his problems in the same manner he'd
always handled major projects: exhaustive research. Using
his familiarity with the resources of the main library of the
University of North Dakota in Grand Forks, he began checking out all the literature he could find concerning organized
crime in the United States.

Several books by famous Mafia defectors who had
turned state's evidence and received new identities from the
Federal Witness Protection Program were of particular interest. In addition, he spent scores of hours in the microfilm
library, reading old *New York Times, Miami Herald, Boston
Globe, Chicago Tribune, Los Angeles Times, New Orleans
Times-Picayune,* and *Minneapolis Star Tribune* articles. The
most valuable sources, however, were the publications of the
FBI and the Department of Justice's organized crime strike
force. Of particular interest were schematics of the major

Mafia families throughout the country. Raven paid particular attention to the makeup of the Cerrillo family in Brooklyn and Manhattan and the Los Angeles crime syndicate. As he reviewed the legitimate activities of the Los Angeles families, he studied their involvement in banking and extortion of the importers and exporters on the waterfront, Cousin Carl's family business.

Another activity occupied hundreds of hours throughout the winter: work in the gunsmith shop in his basement. Working with his hands always gave Raven pleasure, and his current unusual task absorbed even greater concentration than normal. He spent most of his time modifying two weapons, his .270 Winchester deer rifle and the little Ruger 10/22 carbine. Basically, the work consisted of breaking down both firearms into components that could be carried through airport X-ray machines as parts of two pieces of luggage, a briefcase and a garment bag. In addition, with parts bought at machine shops, Raven made silencers for both weapons. The barrels were shortened, with the major reduction being made to the .270. The barrels became the frame at the top of the garment bag. Raven concluded that one butt plate and stock assembly would work for both weapons.

After some experimentation, he decided that a standard stock assembly of hardwood was unnecessary and could be supplanted with only a butt plate snapped on a tubular frame. With a series of joints and welds on the tubular stock assembly, he made one stock that worked for both weapons and could become the frame of his briefcase. The butt plate was covered with leather and became one of the handles on the garment bag.

The bolt assemblies, trigger assemblies, and magazines (particularly the ingenious rotary magazine for the Ruger) posed a problem. Then Raven had a flash of inspiration and decided to become a camera buff. Although it pained his Norwegian frugality, by removing all the inner workings of a new Canon AE-1 camera, leaving just the metal outer shell, and doing the same to a light meter and flash attachment, he made a perfect hiding place for all the problem parts. In addition, the Swarovski scope looked natural in the camera bag, which fit into the briefcase. After hours of painstaking practice, he was able to assemble and disassemble both weapons in minutes. He test-fired his modified weapons at different locations throughout the farm, resulting in a satisfying reduction of the predator and rabbit populations.

7

Although Raven was a familiar figure at the main library of the University of North Dakota, he had seldom been to Thormodsgard Law Library. But the publications by and about the organized crime strike force and the FBI were more readily obtained from the law library. As a result, Raven became a curiosity to the law librarian and a number of the female law students. His striking features and wedge-shaped physique always caused comment, and his deeply tanned face and forearms, blue jeans, boots, and tailored Western shirts were a striking contrast from the typical male law student.

On several occasions—while studying the RICO Act (the short name for the Racketeer Influenced and Corrupt Organizations Act) and other laws in the library—Raven had been distracted by a stunning woman, somewhat older than the students, deeply absorbed in her research. The subject of his glances was visiting professor Angela Simone, on leave from New York University School of Law to teach the first-year courses Criminal Law and Criminal Procedure. Her lovely, curly black hair and olive complexion weren't typical among most Minnesota and North Dakota women. And her wardrobe, which she wore as casually as the New York model she had once been, was equally out of place in Grand Forks.

Angela had been somewhat more discreet in her observations of Raven's powerful hands and forearms and the rippling muscles that occasionally bulged through his jeans and shirt. However, no opportunity had yet provided either of these two proud, independent people to make the other's acquaintance.

Then one day as Raven returned a volume containing the charts of the family trees of the organized crime families, carefully prepared by Flash Maruska, fate intervened in the form of the librarian.

"Oh, Professor Simone," the librarian called. "The book you've been waiting for is back."

Angela walked quickly to the desk as Raven checked in the charts.

"I was beginning to wonder who G. Ravendal was," Angela commented when she saw the date-due slip affixed to the volume Raven was holding. "I assumed he was either another professor or an unregistered auditor of my classes. Might I be so presumptuous as to inquire why you're so interested in the charts of the Crime Commission?"

Up to this point, Angela, aware of the effect her appearance always seemed to elicit from her law students, hadn't yet looked Raven full in the face. But she was accustomed to looking men straight in the eye when speaking to them, and as Raven turned to reply, their eyes met for the first time, and their forearms accidentally brushed together. As Angela looked into his piercing, bright-gray eyes, she felt a completely foreign sensation. Uncharacteristically, as her pulse quickened and her face flushed, Angela dropped her eyes to her forearms. To her dismay, she saw that they were covered with goose bumps and the black hairs of her forearm were raised. *This will not do!* she scolded herself. Finally, years of controlling her emotions in the courtroom as an assistant prosecuting attorney and in the classroom as a law professor took over, and she returned Raven's gaze confidently.

"I'm really a stranger to the law school and this library," said Raven, smiling. "I don't know if you're from this part of the country, but as you've undoubtedly heard, our winters tend to run a little long. Last year, I was studying archaeology and Clovis culture, because I found some Clovis points on my farm. This year, for some reason I've gotten curious about organized crime in the United States."

His explanation only heightened Angela's curiosity. In addition, as she looked again into those gray eyes, tiny points of light seemed to be flashing inside her brain, and she began feeling incredibly powerful, magnetic currents of attraction toward this strangely troubling man. His physical strength seemed to exude from his body. Angela had always appreciated physically powerful men, but thus far in her life, they had been urban men, not nearly as direct as Raven. And certainly not attired in a Western shirt, Levi's, and boots. "What are Clovis points?"

"Clovis points are extremely well-honed spear and arrow tips napped by the Clovis people eleven to thirteen thousand years ago. They hunted down the last of the mammoths and other great mammals out here on the high plains. The best research indicates they probably came originally from Eastern Siberia, across the Bering Land Bridge. From what I've found on my place, I'd say they were wonderfully clever hunters," explained Raven. "Wait a minute. Must I be subjected to a cross-examination right here in the library?"

Angela smiled back at his contagious grin. *God, look at those beautiful white teeth*, she thought. "No, I suppose not. Forgive me for being so inquisitive."

"That's not what I meant at all. I just thought, rather than standing here talking in a library and bothering all the students, maybe we ought to go have a cup of coffee. In answer to your initial question, though, the *G* stands for *Gunar*. But my friends call me Raven."

"Well, Raven, I can't think of anything I'd rather do. Compared to my overwhelmed first-year students, you're a breath of fresh air!"

The librarian, who had been observing their exchange, had also been eyeing Raven for the past several weeks. She angrily cleared her throat. Raven looked at her and apologized. "Sorry, ma'am. I'll try to be quieter next time," he said, aiming a sidelong grin at Angela.

Angela attempted to stifle a giggle and failed with a snort. The librarian's eyebrows shot upward, and Raven and Angela suppressed their laughter, which brought tears to their eyes as they shook with mirth.

Again, Angela was confused. *God, I can't believe I'm acting like this!* she thought. *I haven't felt like this since high school!*

Raven, on the other hand, was becoming somewhat confused himself. Used to being in complete control, he thought, *Better be careful, old scout. The last woman who made you feel like this was Beverly.* Nevertheless, he flushed with pleasure when Angela linked her arm in his as they headed down to the student union. As their forearms touched, both felt the hair rising on their arms.

I wonder if I dare look into those eyes again or if my own eyes will give away too much, thought Angela. *But I want to see them again!*

Over coffee, Angela explained how she came to North Dakota after beginning her career as a prosecutor and then returning to NYU School of Law as a professor. Her humorous descriptions of the differences between law students in New York and Grand Forks soon had them both laughing.

Raven told her about his farming operation and how he loved providing wildlife habitat in conjunction with farming—through beaver dams, artificial impoundments, stocking the ponds with trout, and his wild-grass prairie project.

"You know, I've never been on a real, working farm," said Angela.

"Well, it certainly can be arranged."

When Angela asked about the Ravendal farm's location, he explained that it was next to the Canadian border, about ninety-five miles northeast of Grand Forks.

"How far is it from Winnipeg?"

"Only about seventy-five miles. Why?"

"Well, in two weeks, I'm supposed to give a lecture on the RICO Act to the Manitoba Bar Association. Since you're interested in organized crime, perhaps you'd like to hear how the Anti-Racketeering Act works."

"I'd enjoy that. And maybe you'd like to see my farm sometime during your trip."

"I'd love it! Do you have horses?"

Raven's heart stopped a moment. Then, gazing directly into Angela's dark-brown eyes, he told her, "As a matter of fact, I have two horses, my bay gelding and an Appaloosa mare, who has never been ridden by anyone but a girl. Perhaps I'll tell you the story of the Appaloosa when we meet again. Which reminds me, I've got to get back to my farm before it gets too dark. I'll look forward to meeting you in Winnipeg. Is your lecture in the morning or afternoon?"

After working out the logistics, Raven and Angela simultaneously began to stammer good-bye. Then stopped. Then started again, and finally burst out laughing.

At last, taking her hand, he said, "Till Winnipeg."

"Till Winnipeg," said Angela.

He walked away, his face flushed. Angela watched him go, thinking, *I can't believe this!*

As Raven walked from the student union toward his truck, he also found himself thinking, *I can't believe this!*

8

February 1977

Each time Raven fed and curried the Appaloosa, he thought of Kari, Cousin Carl, and the vile network of drugs, prostitution, extortion, and other crime that had invaded his family. Never a man of conventional morality, Raven kept to his own personal code. In the past, when his personal code had run afoul of stupidity in the establishment, there had been clashes, most of which he had won. These earlier clashes had usually centered around his unique concepts of land use, soil conservation, water impoundments, and hunting or trapping regulations. Fortunately for Raven, he'd always lived in a sparsely settled area. Whenever the pressures of civilization had grown intolerable, he would head for the Northwest Territories or Alaska.

His research into organized crime and its strength in many parts of the United States merged Raven's personal grief and rage with his fierce intellect. As he read newspaper accounts of how top mafiosi continued to run their empires from prison on those rare instances when they were convicted, he began to realize how seldom the law really hurt the top of these organizations. Something elemental in his nature had been stirred, and he began planning his campaign with the same implacable intensity that characterized Norsemen centuries before as they carefully hewed out their long boats to wend their ways up the rivers and over the oceans of the world.

His weaponry prepared, Raven launched his next strike. Leaving his Ramcharger at the Grand Forks airport, he purchased a ticket to Chicago in his own name. His pulse quickened somewhat as he watched his briefcase and garment bag pass through the airport monitor. Since nothing inside had a suspicious shape, however, everything went through without incident. Arriving at O'Hare, he used cash to purchase a ticket to New York's Kennedy Airport in the name of John Farrel. Again, his luggage passed the airport monitors without difficulty. Three hours later, he took an airport taxi to the large, old hotel in Midtown Manhattan where he'd stayed before. He checked in as Peter Berg from Los Angeles, California, and paid cash in advance for five nights' lodging.

Before leaving home, he'd asked Lorne and Little Lars to look after the animals. He said he had to go to Chicago on business and would be back in about a week. Accustomed to Raven's absences during the winter months, nothing seemed unusual to them.

Alone in his Manhattan hotel room, Raven considered his strategy. His research into the Cerrillo family revealed that Dominick had risen to its head through a unique blend of savagery and cunning. He also learned that his brother, Ronnie, a law-school graduate and the family socialite, was a major force, persuading Dom to avoid the violence that had already brought him two short prison terms. With the suave, popular Ronnie advising Dominick, the Cerrillo family had managed to avoid much of the bad publicity that proved so damaging to other New York crime families. Dom's son, Vito, posed another problem. His entry into the prostitution business was no accident; Vito had always been known for his sexual excesses.

Raven viewed the Cerrillo family as a small army, to be attacked as intelligently and effectively as possible. Consequently, even though his desire for revenge was focused mainly on Vito and Dom, he believed he could wreak more havoc with an initial attack on Ronnie. The next day, he began stalking the Cerrillos, focusing his primary attention on Ronnie. Driving a rented car, he followed Ronnie's black Lincoln Town Car from the offices of Cerrillo Shipping on the Lower West Side, taking Interstate 478 around the tip of Manhattan and through the Brooklyn-Battery Tunnel to Ronnie's residence in Brooklyn. To Raven's amazement, Ronnie had grown overconfident. With a casual self-assurance, he dropped his bodyguard-chauffeur five blocks from his home and then drove the Town Car into the driveway of his town house and walked openly to the front door.

Leaving Brooklyn, Raven went next to the sleazy area around Times Square in search of his next quarry, Vito. Knowing that it was a long shot that he'd find Dom's son actually out on the front lines of prostitution, Raven was about to give up for the night when a newspaper article flashed to mind: a photograph of Dom and Vito in a restaurant in Little Italy that was reportedly owned by the family.

Raven drove to the restaurant, found a place at the bar, and ordered a beer. Dressed in gabardine slacks, an open-throated white shirt, and a tweed sport coat, he didn't stand out in the crowd. He made it plain he was interested in a high-class hooker who was quietly working the evening crowd. As he let his gaze drift around the restaurant, he felt his stomach muscles tighten when he spotted Vito in a plush, red-leather booth near the rear, obviously under the influence, permitting himself to be pawed by two equally tipsy young hookers.

The bartender, a clean-cut, collegiate-looking young man, watched Raven's eyebrows go up and commented, "Don't get any ideas, pal. The man owns this place—and the ladies."

Raven shrugged, smiled, and finished his beer. With luck, tomorrow night could prove wonderfully successful. If the timing was right.

Returning to the hotel, he assembled the .270 with the silencer and slid it into the long pocket sewn inside the olive Loden coat he'd purchased long ago in Minneapolis. The coat had been modified to hold the weapon, hidden out of sight, in a long, zippered holster that extended below the left armpit.

Only one task remained for tomorrow: acquiring untraceable transportation. Raven had observed various parking lots and parked vehicles throughout the day and was prepared to act early the next morning, should the opportunity present itself. The badly mud-smeared Wisconsin plates he'd acquired earlier that winter from a junkyard in Superior, Wisconsin, were in his briefcase.

Satisfied that he'd done all he could on his first day, Raven stretched out in bed. After a fitful period, marked by dreams of Kari's death, the morgue, the funeral, Cousin Carl's mangled fingers, and the grinning face of Vito Cerrillo, he willed himself to sleep by focusing his attention on the exact details of his beaver ponds, wild-grass prairie, and woods.

The following morning dawned as one of those rare smogless New York days with a bracing breeze and high cumulus clouds. There was a touch of spring in the February air, although a few piles of gray ice still stood on the corners. Returning his rented vehicle to a midtown agency, Raven took a taxi down to the garment district. There he strolled unobtrusively, looking for an opportunity. He passed up several idling taxis and courier vans as too obvious. As he sipped a cup of coffee in a corner café, a chance finally presented itself. An out-of-town buyer, obviously driving a rental car, had circled the crowded block twice. Finally, in exasperation, he double-parked at the curb, leaving his flashers on.

Raven donned his skintight, black-leather shooting gloves. After waiting a minute to ensure the driver was engaged inside, he quickly checked the driver's door and found it open. He immediately went under the dash and, with knowledge gained from years of working with vehicles on the farm, hotwired the car and drove it away. Nobody on the bustling street seemed to pay any attention.

Twelve blocks away, he stopped the car on a quiet street. Using the screwdriver from his briefcase, he quickly exchanged the dirty Wisconsin plates for the New York plates. He then scraped the decals of the rental company off the windshield and rear bumper with his knife. Next, he drove to a locksmith's shop, where he paid cash to have an impression taken and new keys made for the car.

With several hours on his hands, he decided to head again to the Lower West Side to observe the principals of the Cerrillo business from a safe distance. In midafternoon, a steel-gray Cadillac limousine pulled up to the curb. A chauffeur-bodyguard emerged from the right-front seat and took a position near the right-rear fender. Finally, after another minute or so, the chauffeur opened the left-rear door, and a stocky, muscular figure in a gray topcoat with black-velvet collar and gray homburg emerged. An air of command exuded from the figure—it was discernible even from Raven's vantage point a block away. An attack on this chieftain would require greater care than an attack on his less paranoid brother and son . . . which happened to fit exactly into Raven's plan.

In the late afternoon, the Lincoln Town Car again pulled up to the curb to pick up Ronnie Cerrillo. This time, Raven took a calculated risk, based on the assumption that he knew where the Town Car was going. He kept about a block lead on the Town Car all the way across Manhattan. When he glimpsed the Town Car entering the Brooklyn-Battery Tunnel behind him, he sped up, drove swiftly to Ronnie's neighborhood, and found a parking place along the curb, approximately fifty yards from Ronnie's town house. Reaching into the back seat, he slipped the .270 from its zippered pocket in the Loden coat and surveyed the street. He carefully swept the street in both directions for several minutes. Determining that he wasn't being observed, he made a test sighting through the scope on the corner bricks of the town house. There were no shadow or lighting problems, and the bricks stood out distinctly in the scope.

Raven opened the driver's-side window moments before the Town Car pulled into the driveway. As Ronnie emerged from his car, Raven found him in the scope and elected to make a head shot. A warrior's calmness came over him, and he felt no more emotion than when he exterminated coyotes and foxes on the farm. As Ronnie stepped into the line between Raven and the corner of the town house, Raven locked his breath for steadiness and squeezed off one round. Equipped with the silencer, the weapon emitted a spitting sound as the 160-grain slug crashed into Ronnie Cerrillo's skull, just in front of the left temple. Instantly, the opposite side of the skull exploded, and small fragments of bone and brain splattered the sidewalk and wall.

Thus far, no one had observed or heard anything unusual. Raven placed the rifle on the floor of the car and drove off at a moderate speed. He turned right at the first corner and headed out of Brooklyn, taking the Brooklyn Bridge back to Manhattan. With luck, he might find Vito Cerrillo at the restaurant before the alarm spread.

When he reached Manhattan, Raven pulled onto a side street and disassembled the .270, replacing its barrel into the garment bag and the trigger, magazine, and bolt assemblies into the hollowed-out camera. He then swiftly assembled the smaller Ruger 10/22, into which he slipped the removable cylindrical ten-shot magazine, filled with ten .22 long rifle shells. Weeks before, using his tiniest drill bit, he'd drilled holes into the lead bullets of each shell, effectively turning them into hollow points. Thus drilled, they would mushroom upon impact rather than penetrate, thereby causing far greater tissue damage.

He slipped the Ruger into the zippered pocket of the Loden coat and proceeded to the restaurant. Leaving the coat with the weapon in it hidden on the floor of the back seat, Raven locked the car and casually strolled into the restaurant. Seating himself at the bar, he ordered a beer. He was pleased to note that there was a different bartender on duty from the previous night. He let his gaze drift around the restaurant. Vito's booth of the previous evening was empty.

After sipping his beer for about five minutes, Raven began to feel an increasing tension. Certainly, the alarm would soon be sounded throughout the Cerrillo family. The nature of the shooting would probably cause them to believe they'd been hit by rivals. Within only fractions of an hour, the alarm would spread. In all likelihood, the entire family would "go to the mattresses" in predetermined safe houses throughout New York City and suburbs. Raven decided to risk ordering one more beer. Then he waited, all his nerves sensing danger.

Just as Raven finished his second beer, wondering if he should leave town now, Vito Cerrillo strolled in, accompanied by two black men, both nattily turned out in six hundred–dollar suits, sporting various pinkie and other rings.

Apparently, a business conference was about to begin. As they seated themselves in the same booth as the night before, Raven left and walked swiftly to the car.

Minutes later, with the Loden coat draped over his arm, he reentered the restaurant and proceeded to the men's room. In a toilet stall, he took a ski mask from the pocket of the coat, pulled it over his head, and removed the Ruger. He then put on the coat and walked swiftly to the edge of the main dining room. As he strolled into the room, a few diners noticed him, and gasps arose from the neighboring tables as the patrons began to scatter. When Vito Cerrillo looked up, Raven already had the rifle trained on him. Vito then made a fatal mistake. Rather than dropping below the table, he reached for his gun. As he did, the Ruger spat three times, and three .22 hollow-point slugs crashed into his forehead. The two black men dived beneath the table in panic.

Raven debated for an instant whether or not he'd need to return their fire. Then, swiftly judging that they weren't about to emerge with return fire, he dashed from the restaurant. Still wearing the ski mask, he raced to the car and drove off. In the rearview mirror, he saw several figures on the sidewalk. He concluded that he didn't dare drive the car very long. Traffic was heavy as Raven pulled the ski mask from his face and headed down toward the Battery.

With his heart pounding, he pulled onto a side street. Using the glow of a streetlight, Raven swiftly disassembled the Ruger and placed its components back in their hiding places. He then hung the Loden coat in the garment bag, took a screwdriver from the briefcase, checked both directions, and deftly swapped the license plates back to the car's original New York plates. Raven stepped away from the car, peeling off the skintight gloves he had been wearing ever since he'd "borrowed" the car that morning.

He walked to a busy intersection. After about five minutes, he succeeded in hailing a cab. Traffic was congested all the way out Interstate 78 to Kennedy. Rather than engaging in conversation with the cabbie, Raven feigned sleep. After buying a ticket to O'Hare in the name of Robert Schmidt, he stopped in one of the airport lounges. The flight wasn't scheduled to leave for two hours. He ordered a beer and some peanuts. He then picked up a discarded *Wall Street Journal*, turned to the commodities section, and tried to read the grain and livestock futures. His eyes couldn't even focus on the page as the adrenaline released by the events of the past several hours continued to course through his veins. Raven wondered if he looked as conspicuous as he felt. None of the busy travelers seated in the lounge paid him any attention. As he sat there, the evening television news came on, and Raven heard the anchor give the lead story: "Two alleged Mafia leaders slain in apparent gangland war." His attention was drawn to the set, along with that of the other travelers.

As Raven sat watching the evening news broadcast, pandemonium reigned supreme throughout the Cerrillo family.

Dom was issuing orders and reading reports in his plush mahogany-paneled office at Cerrillo Shipping when his cousin Joe Cerrillo stalked into the room. "I got bad news, boss. Some asshole whacked Ronnie!"

Hearing of the death of his beloved brother and confidant, Dominick turned into a raging, snarling animal. "It's gotta be the fucking Gambuccis!" he shouted. He began issuing orders to all the other principals of the family, telling them to avoid the usual places of business and go to assigned safe houses throughout the city. As he was making the calls, his trusted bodyguard, Billy Malone, entered the room with a fearful expression on his face.

"What's the matter with you, Billy, sneaking around like a whipped pup?" snarled the savage Dom.

Afraid of what might happen to the bearer of bad tidings, Billy tried to break the news indirectly. "Afraid we've got some more bad news, Dom."

"Spill it!"

"They got Vito, too, at the restaurant."

An instant later, exactly as he'd feared, Dom leaped on Billy, savagely pistol-whipping him with his automatic. Accustomed to Dom's wild temper, several other members of the family immediately pulled Dom off the helpless Billy.

"Come on, Dom, come on," they pleaded. "Billy didn't do it. Lay off."

Coming to his senses, Dom sat solemnly in his chair, his temper still smoldering. "Sorry, Billy. You know how I get," he finally said through clenched teeth.

"I know, boss," said Billy, gingerly fingering the welts on his face. "I know."

9

ETECTIVES FROM BROOKLYN, MANHATTAN, the Governor's Commission on Organized Crime, and the FBI swarmed over both shooting scenes. However, primary jurisdiction over both cases rested with the respective local police detectives.

Flash Maruska and Henry Grogan, upon hearing the news, coordinated with Charles Hull from the FBI, and by late that night they'd visited both scenes.

"With all the locals, politicians, and state guys, it'll be a miracle if any evidence turns up," Charlie complained. "What have we learned so far?"

"Not much," said Grogan, "except somebody apparently hired some fine shooters."

"Why do you say *shooters*, rather than *shooter?*" asked Maruska.

"Well, we're not sure yet because they only found one slug over in Brooklyn, and the slugs in Manhattan are pretty well mangled," Grogan told them, "but ballistics believes two very different weapons were involved. Apparently, the Brooklyn shooter was using a fairly high-powered weapon, probably with a scope. The witnesses who weren't totally terrified in the restaurant recall a much smaller weapon with open sights. One thing is sure as hell true—the shooter in the restaurant was one hell of a shot."

"Why do you say that?"

"All three shots were in one tight group, about the size of a silver dollar. I saw Vito's forehead—it looks like it was rammed with a triangular-shaped instrument; the shots were that tightly spaced."

"I'll be damned. How about the shooting in Brooklyn, what was the distance there?"

"Apparently about half a block."

"Could the same shooter have made it from Brooklyn to Little Italy in time? What's the fix on the times of the shootings?" Hull asked.

"We don't know the exact time of the Brooklyn shooting. Apparently, they notified the family long before they thought to call the police."

"Typical," Flash reflected.

"If it was an organized pair of hits from another family, probably at least two shooters were involved."

"Yeah," Hull offered, "and there'll probably be hell to pay in the families."

"I'm not absolutely sure," Flash responded. "There's something atypical about these shootings. No automatic weapons were used, and nothing was done at real close range. I'm just not sure."

"Hell," said Hull, "somebody just wised up enough to hire out-of-town specialists, that's all."

"Yeah, you're probably right," Flash conceded. Still, something seemed wrong to the gentle giant. There was a flavor about this situation that ran contrary to the gangland hits he'd observed during his entire professional life. These shootings would bear watching. "One thing I think we can all count on—it's going to be damned interesting to see how the families react."

While this conversation was taking place among the investigators, Raven arrived at Chicago O'Hare, where he took a taxi downtown between flights. Walking around Chicago's Old Town with his briefcase and garment bag, he reached a darkened street corner. He stopped, removed the Wisconsin license plates from the briefcase, and left one in a trash can. Walking swiftly on, he threw the other into another receptacle a block away. He then hailed a taxi back to O'Hare in time for his flights to Minneapolis–St. Paul and Grand Forks.

Two days earlier than his forecast to Lorne and Little Lars, Raven drove the Ramcharger into the farmyard, reentered the farmhouse, hung up his clothes, cleaned and oiled both weapons, and returned them to their hiding places deep in his closet. He changed into blue jeans and headed out to the stable to look after the horses. The little Appaloosa walked up to him, so he patted her neck and gave her some oats. As he turned the animals out into the corral, he gazed across the grove at the early-morning sky.

"I know it can never bring you back, Kari," he murmured softly. "But at least we did something about it. We didn't just sit here and take it."

10

Back in New York City, Joey Gambucci, head of the Gambucci family, was in a state of near panic. It was true that there was no love lost between the Gambuccis and Cerrillos. They'd had bitter jurisdictional fights over some of the labor unions—particularly on the docks on both the New York and Jersey sides—and some conflicts over narcotics. But Joey would never dream of ordering a hit on any of the Cerrillos. Not with that animal Dom heading up the family, not to mention the number of soldiers the Cerrillos could marshal for a war compared to the tightly knit but fewer Gambuccis, who were arguably more youthful and vigorous. But still.

Joey had made his bones by hitting some of the crazy Scuzas years before. The Scuzas, an insurgent, smaller Mob family out of Brooklyn, had been loosely affiliated with the Cerrillos. But everyone had breathed a sigh of relief when Joey had taken out Red Scuza, even Dom. Knowing Dom's tendency to jump to conclusions, and knowing the role Ronnie had always played in calming his rages, Joey reluctantly sent word throughout Gambucci family to be on the alert for attacks from the Cerrillos. He had a growing sense of dread over what would happen if Dom lashed out blindly at his or any other suspected New York family. Retaliation would necessarily follow, and a full-scale war could erupt. That could decimate the Gambuccis or any other family the powerful Cerrillos perceived as a direct challenge.

Joey wondered if a telephone call would do any good, or just make matters worse. All morning, he'd been staring at the telephone, debating. Finally, he dialed Dominick's house. A female voice answered and told him, as he expected, that Dom couldn't be reached at home.

"Just tell him Joey Gambucci called to offer him his sincere regrets. Tell Dom I'd like to talk to him . . . that I'll help in any way I can." After receiving his promise that the message would be passed to Dom, Joey told his secretary to send the biggest, most expensive floral arrangements she could buy over to the homes of Ronnie, Vito, and Dom Cerrillo. Then he headed for the gun locker in his office, taking out a Walther automatic with a shoulder holster, which he put on, plus an Uzi submachine gun. He then sent for his bodyguard and an armored car, collected his brother Luca "Lucky" Gambucci and his cousin Sergio, and ordered the armored limousine to drive to the fortified family farm in New Jersey.

I wonder what we ought to do about the funerals? he thought as the limousine left the city and headed for the farm.

11

THE IMPENDING JOINT FUNERAL FOR Ronnie and Vito Cerrillo was shaping into a media and law-enforcement extravaganza. Ever since the shootings, the tabloids had been running screaming headlines about Mob warfare springing up again in New York City. Television crews were posted nonstop at Ronnie's and Vito's homes and at the Cerrillo headquarters in lower Manhattan. Not to be outdone, the more dignified dailies began giving the Mafia, particularly the New York families, front-page treatment. All the major networks were running features on the Mob in America. Erudite and less-than-erudite columnists and TV commentators pontificated ad infinitum on the issues of criminal law enforcement, organized crime, drugs, labor racketeering, bookmaking, extortion, counterfeiting, prostitution, and contract murder. The NYPD, New York's state attorney general's office, the FBI, and the Justice Department strike force all made separate—and in some cases, joint—plans for surveillance of the funeral.

Flash Maruska and Henry Grogan were deeply involved in the surveillance conducted by the strike force. The cynical Henry commented, "Gonna be quite a circus, Flash."

Maruska agreed. "All the politicians want in on the act. And all the families are afraid not to attend for fear of antagonizing crazy Dom. All it means from our standpoint is nothing is gonna break until after the funeral. After that, there are even odds on whether or not this thing is going to erupt into something wilder."

12

ACK AT THE FARM, RAVEN WATCHED AND READ the media reports with grim satisfaction. After he returned home, he devoted himself to farm business, which always picked up in the months before planting. There was equipment to get into shape, although Lorne nearly always kept everything in excellent running order. More important, there was the matter of deciding which crops to seed on their many fields. His evenings were spent in the gunsmith shop, preparing the weapons for his next strike. If his plans were to blossom properly, different weaponry was needed. As he toiled at his workbench, disquieting thoughts along an entirely different line sometimes came to mind—a lovely law professor and what the reaction of such a sophisticated woman would be to his farm.

Two weeks later, Raven had completed his plans and selected his weapons. He'd continued to follow the news from New York, hoping the unstable Dom might erupt without more encouragement. Thus far the scene had been quiet. From his studies of the New York families, Raven knew the Gambuccis would be Dom's primary suspects because of their past conflicts and the overlap of their operations in labor racketeering and narcotics. Both families had strong ties in Florida, connections for Colombian cocaine and marijuana. He considered striking next in Florida in an effort to spread the flames of war as widely and quickly as possible. But the Florida drug scene was so violent, disorganized, and wild that there was a strong possibility any efforts in Miami would be interpreted as just more of the usual crazy, random violence. Also, the insurgent Colombians and Cubans in Florida were another complicating factor that made it difficult to orchestrate a hit to have maximum impact on the national Mafia.

Raven concluded another trip to New York was his best option. His first trip taught him that his greatest challenge was securing reliable, untraceable transportation without running the risk of being arrested for car theft. The main problem was that any vehicle rented in his own name required the use of his driver's license. Thus, if an automobile had to be abandoned because of an unforeseen emergency, it could be directly traced to him. Using a stolen vehicle and stolen plates left no possibility of a trace, but the risk of being caught snatching a vehicle was substantial. He finally decided that buying junk plates was the wisest course; it was easily done without revealing his identity. The most useful tool, though, would be an alternate valid driver's license, preferably from another state. As he pondered his *Official Airline Guide* and a map of the northeastern United States, a plan finally came to mind.

Raven told Lorne he'd be out of town for a few days. He then drove again to the airport at Grand Forks. He was purchasing airline tickets to Chicago in his own name when he sensed a presence nearby. Glancing about, his heart stopped as his eyes met those of Angela Simone. For an instant they both paused, and Angela's lips parted. Suddenly, they were clasping hands and all the electricity he remembered from their first meeting returned.

"What brings a busy farmer to the airport?"

Raven thought furiously. "I'm heading out to Cornell to meet with some agronomy professors about some new seed varieties," he lied, hoping it didn't sound too odd. "What brings you to the airport?"

"Oh, I had some unfinished business at NYU. I'm just returning. I hope you're still planning to come to my lecture in Winnipeg next week," she added, feeling a little giddy and hoping she didn't sound too eager.

"Of course. I've been counting on hearing your lecture and showing you the farm," he replied, grateful for the change of subject but disturbed that he sounded like a schoolboy again.

After an exchange of other pleasantries, they parted, both excited.

Raven willed himself back to the business at hand. This trip, he hadn't taken the specialized garment bag or briefcase. Instead, although it hurt him to do it, he had taken his old Remington 12-gauge and cut it down to a sawed-off shotgun, chopping the barrel to the shortest possible length. He modified the stock to a pistol grip. Memories of duck hunting with his father had flooded back as he transformed the trusty old shotgun from one that conjured only good memories to a weapon of war. A weapon in an undeclared war, which Raven felt was appropriate. *Do they give any warning before they strike? Did they warn my family before they began their rape and plunder? I'll give exactly the same warning—none.*

Over the centuries, aggressors and plunderers have always made their own rules. The laws of ordered society have generally been insufficient in the face of calculated sneak attacks. And occasionally over the ages, vengeance has been wrought by avengers, using the same methodology as the barbaric terrorist. The laws of men work inefficiently at best in times of peace. In times of war, as the saying goes, it's time to put on the mantle of the tiger.

On this mission, Raven wouldn't keep his weapons in his carry-ons. He placed the carefully wrapped component parts of the chopped shotgun into a steel toolbox, along with many other tools, which he then packed in the bottom of a suitcase, surrounded by coveralls, his skintight gloves, and other clothing. He checked this bag through to Chicago, taking a ticket in his own name. In Chicago, he rented a car at the airport, took Interstate 90 through the loop and out to South Chicago and Hammond, Indiana. There he cruised the auto-salvage yards until he found a dealer willing to sell a set of plates from a wrecked car for cash, no questions asked. After stashing the plates in his luggage, he drove the rental car back to the airport. He paid cash at the United counter for a ticket to Philadelphia in the name of Charles Derby. In Philadelphia, he took a taxi to a gas station in a working-class neighborhood of South Philly, not far from the naval shipyard. In the restroom of the gas station, he donned coveralls and work boots. Then he headed for a workingman's bar. Sipping a beer, he surveyed the patrons. After a few minutes, he saw what he was looking for. Raven approached a tall, rough-looking laborer who seemed intent on happily consuming all his wages. The man was definitely tipsy.

"Buy you a beer?"

"Sure, why the hell not—maybe I'll have some money for the old lady when I get home," growled the stranger.

After another beer, Raven and his new "friend" began playing liars' poker with dollar bills. Raven kept buying beers for the stranger, whose condition steadily worsened. He feigned drunkenness along with the stranger. After about an hour, the opportunity he'd been waiting for presented itself. Slapping his billfold on the bar, the man told Raven, "Get us another round while I'm gone, buddy. Gotta go water my horse." With that, he lurched off the stool toward the men's room.

Raven casually took the man's billfold and flipped through it. Sandwiched in the middle of some photographs, a union card, and other identification, he located the man's driver's license. When no one was looking, he slipped it into his pocket. He then casually returned the billfold to the bar. Soon the new "friend" reappeared. After another round, Raven excused himself. Claiming he had urgent business, he picked up his briefcase and strolled out into the street.

Within minutes, he hailed a cab and headed immediately for a downtown rental-car agency. There, using his newly acquired Pennsylvania driver's license, he checked out a medium-size car. Before entering the car, he again donned his leather gloves. Within fifteen minutes, he'd crossed the Ben Franklin Bridge, passed through Camden, New Jersey, and was headed northeast on the New Jersey Turnpike. Driving through the wastelands of oil refineries and heavy industry on the Jersey side of the water as darkness fell, he pulled into a rest area. Opening his suitcase, he pulled out the Indiana plates and a screwdriver and then switched the plates.

He found a cheap motel in Jersey City and checked in under the name of George Parsons of Gary, Indiana, giving no street address. It was the kind of motel where street addresses and names were of little import. As Raven paid cash in advance for two days' lodging, the night clerk's eyebrows arched, and he smirked knowingly as he handed over the key. Raven smiled back at him and left for the sanctuary of his room. There, as he unpacked his luggage and began checking weapons, he turned on the evening news. The topic of organized crime, so hot only a week ago, seemed to have cooled down to a mere mention of the fact that the New York families seemed to be quiet after the Cerrillo funeral. Raven removed the plug from the 12-gauge so its magazine would hold five double-aught buckshot shells. He then placed twenty more shells in a bandolier belt designed to be worn diagonally across the chest. Smiling grimly, he muttered, "We'll see how long it stays quiet."

Satisfied that he'd done everything possible for the evening, he watched the remainder of the evening news. Then he channel-hopped, hoping to find a program that would put him to sleep. One channel was showing a Mafia film about a legendary figure from the 1930s renowned for his savagery. Raven watched it for a while, marveling at how the saga of violence and treachery echoed his research into Dominick Cerrillo. *Maybe history doesn't always have to repeat itself,* he mused. *Maybe sometimes, one enraged citizen can make a difference.* With this thought in mind, he drifted off to sleep. He slept a warrior's sleep, dreaming of battles centuries ago, of long boats, and of Vikings being borne on their shields in death to Valhalla.

13

R AVEN AWOKE TO A FIERCE AND BLUSTERY DAY. Hard northeast winds drove diagonal, slashing sheets of rain. Occasional gusts even pushed the rain parallel to the ground. Driving the car away from the motel, he turned again toward the refineries, found a truck stop, and forced himself to eat a breakfast of fried eggs, bacon, toast, and coffee.

Leaving the restaurant, he pulled his car to the back of the parking lot, reached into the back seat for his suitcase, and opened it on the front seat beside him. He removed the sawed-off shotgun, the bandolier of shells, a fatigue jacket with holster modified to hold the shotgun inside at waist level, a navy stocking cap, and a Richard Nixon Halloween mask, modified with enlarged eye holes and heavy elastic bands to hold it in place. He stuffed his regular jacket into the suitcase, slung the bandolier of shells across his chest, and donned the fatigue jacket and stocking cap. He put the shotgun and mask back in the suitcase, which he left partially unzipped. He drove at a leisurely pace toward the Hoboken docks until he reached the headquarters of Longshoremen's Local 37A, a corrupt union branch he'd studied in intense detail. From his studies, Raven knew the Gambucci family hierarchy regularly met there.

Trucks rumbled down the street from both directions as he drove slowly by the union hall. The nondescript, yellow-brick structure with glass-block windows was totally monolithic from the outside. A frontal attack would probably be fruitless. The absence of shops and people in the vicinity created another problem. A lone car, parked at the curb, was certain to draw attention. Raven drove slowly away.

About ten blocks from the hall, he found a small café. He bought a large Styrofoam container of coffee and a bag of doughnuts, went back to the car, and cruised past Local 37A again. Circling the block, coming back from the opposite direction this time, he noticed two Cadillac limousines parked near the rear door. Rain continued to lash the street, running in streams across the parking lot. Occasional gusts of wind shook his car as he pulled up beside a Dumpster in the alley at the far corner of the parking lot. He removed the stocking cap, put the Halloween mask on top of his head, and set the sawed-off shotgun beside him. He then began his vigil, checking his rearview mirror regularly as he sipped his coffee and munched on the doughnuts.

Finally, at eleven forty-five, the back door of the union hall opened. The burly figure of a Gambucci soldier emerged to check the area. Heavy rain pelted him in the face, and he failed to notice the car idling beside the Dumpster. He ducked back inside the door and shouted something to someone farther back. As the door swung open and two more figures stepped outside, Raven started the car rolling slowly down the alley. As two more figures emerged from the door, he reached the point closest to the door of the union hall. A space of about thirty yards separated him from the Gambuccis. The five men were just about to enter the limousines as he pulled the mask over his face, flung open the door, and began racing across the parking lot. At about twenty yards, his presence was detected, but within a couple of seconds he covered another ten yards and fired two blasts of the shotgun. The shots cut down the two nearest men. The figure at the driver's side of the farthest car hit the ground as the two remaining figures bolted for the door of the building.

Dropping to one knee, Raven let the gun roar again. The blast of the shotgun caught the rear man as he entered the door, and several stray pellets also hit the man in front of him. Dropping to his side on the wet parking lot, Raven directed his last shot beneath the cars, sweeping the ground. It caught the figure crouching on the far side of the second car in the thighs and crotch. Raven then quickly grabbed three more shells from the bandolier and jacked them into the gun as he ran toward the open door of his car.

Just as he was feeling safe, he felt a sharp blow on his right shoulder and heard the crack of a pistol. He lurched into the car and sped away. As he drove madly through the driving rain, his right shoulder began to stiffen. He felt the warm trickle of blood running over his shoulder and down his side, soaking his shirt. By the time he was a mile away, sharp pain shot through his shoulder, and he began to feel dizzy. He opened the window of the driver's side and let the rain hit him in the face. He knew he couldn't go much farther without stanching the flow of blood, which had now noticeably seeped through his fatigue jacket.

After about five miles, Raven pulled into a gas station and stepped shakily out of the car. The shock of the rain in his face revived him momentarily. Rain continued to beat on him as he tried the men's room door. It was locked! He tried the women's room, found it open, and stepped inside. As he locked the door, he spotted a sanitary-napkin dispenser on the wall. His right arm refused to pull back far enough to get at the change in the right pocket of his Levi's. In desperation, he tore the entire dispenser off the wall with his left hand. Packages of sanitary napkins spilled out over the floor. He struggled out of his fatigue jacket. He touched the wound with his left hand and was relieved to find that the bullet had only grazed the back of the shoulder before ripping a shallow furrow through the muscle and tissue and exiting at the upper right point of his shoulder. He felt threads of cloth embedded in the wound and knew it had to be cleaned before long.

Ripping open one of the sanitary napkin packages with his teeth, he placed a wad of several napkins on the wound and then pressed against the wall to slow the bleeding. Some of the drowsiness was returning. Raven felt a twinge of shock as he saw the small pool of blood on the floor. With his left hand, he removed his belt, looped its end through the buckle, and pulled it as tightly as he could bear, drawing the sanitary napkins into the wound. He then proceeded to loop the belt around the compress several times and tucked the end through the last loop, pulling it as tightly as he could. With great difficulty, he got his left arm back into the fatigue jacket and flipped it over his shoulder. He knelt down and filled the fatigue jacket pockets with packages of sanitary napkins.

Reeling, Raven staggered out the door to the car and managed to get the key into the ignition. Everything seemed to be moving in slow motion. As he pulled out of the station, he noticed two women entering the ladies' room. Apparently startled by the bloody mess he'd left behind, they looked toward him as he pulled out onto the highway and drove off.

Five minutes later, Raven felt himself blacking out. He pulled onto the shoulder of the highway and finally passed out at the wheel as the traffic zoomed past. Images of mutilated bodies and faces flashed through his brain as the blackness descended upon him.

Back at the union hall, pandemonium reigned. Various soldiers held defensive positions at the windows as bellows of rage from members of the Gambucci family filled the air. Joey Gambucci, bleeding from the wounds of three shotgun pellets in the back of his neck, was on the phone to his brother Lucky. The corpses of two of his soldiers—slender and handsome Tony "Rocker" Scalia and the huge Jimmy the Bull— lay in the rear entry where they'd been dragged. Worse yet, Sergio Gambucci, the older driver of the far car, had taken a direct blast across the thigh, groin, and genitals and was lying unconscious in the entryway. Several of the union employees tried to administer first aid.

Joey yelled, "Lucky, I knew that fucking mad dog Dom was gonna hit us! We should have hit him first. . . . The motherfucker always hated me, ever since the council turned him down and gave us this local. Goddamn it, Luca, I'm bleeding, and I want to spill some Cerrillo blood! If we let him pick away at us, with the number of soldiers he's got, we're dogmeat!"

14

AFTER WHAT SEEMED LIKE HOURS, Raven's eyelids fluttered open, and he realized he was in an impossible position. Actually, he'd only been unconscious for several minutes, but it was only a matter of time before a policeman or someone else stopped and found him. His wound was throbbing, and his breathing was forced as he put the car back in gear and slowly drove off. Keeping the window open to remain awake, Raven finally managed to drive back to the motel. He got the shotgun back into the suitcase, removed the keys from the car, and staggered to the door of the motel room carrying the case. Once again, the rain provided cover. No one was watching as he finally got the key into the lock. As soon as he closed the door, he fell facedown on the bed.

After lying on the bed in the darkened motel room for over an hour, Raven revived again. The wound was throbbing. Dragging himself from bed, he lurched into the bathroom, peeled off the fatigue jacket and ripped shirt, removed the belt and blood-soaked sanitary napkins, and examined his wound. No substantial muscle or bone damage. Apparently, the bullet had been fired at such an oblique angle that it merely nicked the bone and then plowed through the top layer of shoulder muscle before exiting. Raven wondered if the bullet was embedded in the car or if it had ricocheted off elsewhere. The trough plowed by the bullet had left a tiny amount of exposed bone and about three square inches of purplish hematoma. Blood oozed from the furrow.

He knew the greatest danger was shock from continued blood loss. In addition, something had to be done about the risk of infection. Raven carried no antiseptic and dared not appear bleeding in a drugstore. He searched for field expedients in his luggage. He concluded that a compress made of sanitary napkins wouldn't suffice on a long-term basis. Opening a bottle of aftershave lotion with his mouth, he gritted his teeth and poured the lotion into the wound. The alcohol in the lotion stung deeply, further reviving him.

Having thus cleaned the wound, he opened the blade of his buck knife with his teeth. He then filled the sink with crumpled toilet tissue and twisted pages from the Gideon Bible he'd found in the room's bedside table. Using both hands to strike a match, he ignited the mass of papers in the sink. They immediately threw an intense heat. Holding the knife blade into the heart of the flame, Raven turned it over again and again until it was red-hot.

Looking over his shoulder in the mirror, he took the knife in his left hand, gritted his teeth, and cauterized the entire length of the wound with the searing blade. The acrid smell of burnt flesh joined the smell of the burning paper. Raven's eyes teared from the pain of the unanesthetized cauterization. Wiping his eyes, he examined the wound again. He added more paper to the flame, reheated the blade again, checked the mirror, and completed the unpleasant task. His shoulder burning with pain, he flushed the remains of the fire down the sink. He smiled grimly, giving thanks for the cheapness of a motel that didn't install adequate smoke detectors or sprinklers in its rooms.

Returning to the bedroom, Raven used the buck knife and his teeth to cut and tear a number of strips from the sheet on the bed. He opened one of the sanitary napkins, doused it with aftershave lotion, and placed it on the bed. He then tied slipknots in two of the strips of sheet, inserted his arm in the loops, and pulled them up to his shoulder. He set the sanitary napkin on the wound, placed the loops of sheet over the sanitary napkin, pulled them tight, and wrapped them around his shoulder, tucking the ends into his armpit. He then found a sweatshirt in his suitcase, pulled it over his head, threw his remaining belongings in the suitcase, and left the room.

Minutes later, he was back on the New Jersey Turnpike, returning to Philadelphia. As he passed the refineries and storage tanks of New Jersey, he wondered what was happening in the Cerrillo and Gambucci families. A sense of exhilaration at surviving filled him, and he laughed. *I wonder what part of the Gideon Bible I used to cauterize this wound. I'll bet it came from the Old Testament rather than the New!*

Just outside Philadelphia, Raven pulled into the far end of a rest area, opened the trunk, and replaced the car's

Pennsylvania plates. Strolling around the area, he put the Indiana plates in two separate trash containers. He spent that night in a motel near Cherry Hill on the New Jersey side of the Delaware.

The next morning, his sore shoulder reminded him to check his wound. Although there was some oozing of blood and clear liquid from the wound when he removed the sanitary napkin, it appeared that the cauterization had been generally effective. He set another napkin on the wound and fastened it as he had the night before. Then he went to a drive-through and ordered a breakfast special with a large, black coffee.

After Raven completed his breakfast in the car, it was late enough to head for a large supermarket. He purchased a small bottle of disinfectant, some large gauze bandages, a package of gauze, and a roll of adhesive tape. In the restroom of a nearby filling station, he properly cleansed and dressed his wound. An hour later, he checked in the rented automobile. On the street outside the rental agency, he hailed a cab and traveled south to Philadelphia International Airport. By noon, he'd purchased a ticket to Chicago in his own name. By nightfall, he was back in Grand Forks and headed home in the black Ramcharger. As he pushed through the darkness of the lonely northwestern Minnesota highway, he pondered what havoc he'd brought down upon the heads of his enemies.

Back in New Jersey, Joey Gambucci faced a kairotic choice. All generals, if they ever actually enter combat, reach such a crossroads. Retreat and retrenchment gives the enemy time to regroup and strike again. On the other hand, a counterattack, launched from a position of weakness and confusion, can result in total decimation of the fighting force. Joey reflected on his brother's words. Then he considered the disposition and willingness of his soldiers to wage war, and he chose to attack. Little did he know what a surprise the attack would be, or how savagely his men would strike, riding waves of rage caused by the Gambucci deaths.

15

JUSTICE DEPARTMENT STRIKE FORCE HEADQUARTERS and local New York and New Jersey police detectives could have satisfied Raven's speculation about the effect of his actions on his enemies. The day and night had been filled with savage butchery at nearly all Cerrillo family businesses. Dom Cerrillo himself had narrowly escaped death in a bombing and machine-gun attack at Cerrillo headquarters. It had been several hours before he could order the entire family to the mattresses, because the Gambuccis had cut his telephone wires before striking. When Dom was able to reach a phone, he began to telephone Cerrillo family members and friends all along the Eastern Seaboard, calling in his markers from Boston to Miami, demanding hits on all Gambucci operations. He didn't really succeed in prompting any action, though he did get many promises.

Flash Maruska and his staff, upon hearing the news, prepared the equivalent of a war room in their own headquarters. Flash fashioned two new charts, one for each family.

As various members of the strike force offered opinions—generally along the line of "I knew it was a only a matter of time before the violence erupted again"—Maruska ruminated about the possibility that the initial attacks were perpetrated by one man. It seemed odd, based on the sketchy information he had, that Dominick Cerrillo, the head of a powerful Mafia family with many soldiers at his disposal, would order an attack with only one shotgun-wielding hit man.

Stomach growling, Maruska decided to keep his thoughts to himself for the time being. He succumbed to the stress and dialed for a pizza, with the works. It would be quite a while before he'd be home again—so, what the hell.

As the information about the hits came in, Flash marveled at some of the targets. They included bankers, executives, local politicians, restaurateurs, bookmakers, drug dealers— and, of course, union bosses. The prominence of a few of the politicians surprised him. *With an organization so entrenched in legitimate affairs*, he thought, *how will any federal, state, or local prosecutor ever take them down?*

During the days following his return to the farm, Raven immersed himself in preparations for spring planting. Although his wound was sore, he concluded it would heal without medical attention. Checking it in the mirror, he noted with satisfaction that the cauterization was effective; there was no longer any oozing of blood or fluid from the wound. The wound appeared as a dark, mahogany-colored streak on his shoulder, approximately the length and width of his little finger. It had the appearance of a burn, as if he'd somehow accidentally branded himself with a hot, metal rod. He kept the wound covered with a piece of gauze bandage and was able to move his arm normally enough that it didn't cause comment from Lorne, Lars, or Beverly.

The Gambucci attack on the Cerrillos was continuing with a fury that hadn't been seen for many years among the East Coast mafiosi. Knowing the superior size of the Cerrillo family, the Gambuccis decided massive, immediate hits were their only hope. Squads of Gambucci soldiers descended on union halls, bookmaking parlors, drug dealers, numbers operators, and the homes of the Cerrillo crime family all the way from Boston down to Norfolk, Virginia. Only the Miami operations were overlooked because of the logistical problems involved in mounting an attack in that confused, cocaine-laced atmosphere.

The element of surprise had been complete; within three days, twenty-nine members of the Cerrillo family had been killed and eleven more wounded, compared to only one death and three wounded among the Gambuccis. All the families up and down the Eastern Seaboard and along the Gulf Coast were in an uproar by the end of the week since the Cerrillos called in their chits with related families, demanding retaliation against the Gambuccis. Since all members of the warring families had gone to the mattresses, however, communications were difficult.

Police departments in the affected cities were working overtime, as well as the FBI and the Justice Department strike force. Flash Maruska and Henry Grogan spent nearly all their time at the office, receiving information from the various police departments as the stories broke.

"Damn it, Flash, I don't think there's been a war approaching this size since the crazy Gatto Mob tried to take over Brooklyn back in the fifties."

"Yeah, it's a wonderful thing to see. This entire war is gonna play hell with my organizational charts—not to mention all the police investigations about the dead bosses, underbosses, and soldiers. It's a wonder to behold," he mused. "Say, Henry, have you given any more thought to the hits that started this whole party? The rifle killings? Did you follow up on the Brooklyn and Manhattan ballistics investigations of those two hits?"

"Not much to go on, Flash. They never found any brass on the first hit with the large-bore rifle. And the slug plowed into the brick wall of Ronnie Cerrillo's house after it exploded out the far side of his skull, so it was too badly misshapen for ballistics to determine the bore size of the rifle. They think from the weight of the lead that it could have been anything from a .270 up through a .30-06, but all the rifles around that size fire various grain bullets; so without a slug retaining most of its shape, it's impossible to tell the exact bore. Manhattan, on the other hand, found spent brass in the restaurant. The shooter was using .22 longs. Microscopic investigation of the brass seems to indicate it was fired from a new Ruger rotary-magazine .22. And get this—ballistics tells me the slugs mushroomed on impact because tiny holes had been drilled into the lead, making each .22 slug like a hollow point! I never heard of anything like that, have you?"

Flash reflected a moment. "Not lately, Henry. I do recall some stories about deer hunters during World War II, when ammo was rationed, drilling holes in their bullets to increase the shocking power so one hit anywhere on a deer would bring down the animal. I think it's illegal now. It makes you kinda wonder a little bit about the shooter, doesn't it?"

"What do you mean? And why do you say *shooter* rather than *shooters*?"

"I'm not sure, but is just seems a little odd to me that the weaponry in both the Ronnie and Vito Cerrillo hits involved sporting rifles. And both hits apparently involved a crack marksman. Also, the last hit indicates real expertise in doctoring bullets. I mean, it sure as hell doesn't fit a typical Mafia pattern, does it?"

"Do you think the Gambuccis brought in some new contract hitter from the outside?"

"I don't know yet. It just sort of fascinates me how this whole thing seems to have been started by something so abnormal." Privately, Flash had been wondering for some time if someone was out there fulfilling a fantasy he'd entertained for years. It never ceased to amaze him how private citizens permitted the Mob to take control of lives, businesses, and cities without retaliating, even in the face of some of the worst atrocities. He sometimes wondered what the results would be if an aroused group of citizens took direct action rather than trusting the plodding, and often compromised, work of understaffed police forces and prosecuting attorneys. At times, Flash had played out scenarios where enraged groups of citizens stormed the offices of local prosecutors, mayors, and legislators to demand action, and then, when they became frustrated by the bureaucratic inertia, took action themselves. Flash knew the extent to which the citizenry of America is armed. He believed it was a real tribute to the inclination of Americans to abide by the law that there'd never been any real vigilantism directed at something as evil as organized crime. Of course, organized crime is sophisticated and insidious, whenever possible preferring to take over private business through threats rather than direct action. And it expertly uses its great economic power to take advantage of the greed and venality of its victims. *Still,* Flash reflected, *you'd think that once in a while someone who'd been savaged by the Mob would strike back, given the general ineffectiveness of local police forces and prosecutors. Not to mention the out-and-out corruption rife in many communities.*

But Flash was a career member of the law-enforcement community, sworn to oppose vigilantism in all forms. In his youth he'd enjoyed reading about heroic vigilantes on the American frontier before civilization brought law and order. Over the years, as he witnessed the great injustices and human misery caused by organized crime, he'd sometimes fantasized about the impact an intelligent and brave private citizen might have, acting without the fetters of the legal process. He imagined the satisfaction such a man might feel as he repaid, in kind, the violent excesses of the Mob. When he had these fantasies, Flash always felt a little sheepish and guilty afterward. After all, he was a professional, dedicated to upholding the law in all respects. And during his career, he'd observed "cowboy" policemen overstep the boundaries of the law during the course of arrests and investigations, and he knew that these excesses frequently went unreported.

Flash himself had always deplored overreaction and brutality on the part of his fellow officers. On the other hand, when he put himself in the shoes of crime victims, he wondered whether or not he'd be able to restrain himself if ever he or one of his loved ones fell prey to the Mob.

16

THE DAY OF ANGELA SIMONE'S LECTURE to the Manitoba Bar Association, Raven found himself acting in unusual ways. He awoke at dawn picturing the farm as Angela might see it for the first time, making many small adjustments so it would look as good as possible. Until then, he'd cared about appearances solely for his own pleasure. Now, thinking about what Angela might notice, he forked fresh straw into the horses' stalls even though it was several days early, gave the horses an extra currying and rubdown, and even picked some wild flowers and put them in a vase on the kitchen table.

After he crossed through Canadian customs and headed north on the empty highway, he felt as though he were flying. Experiencing a light-headed sort of release that amazed him, he found himself singing as he rushed along the asphalt corridor through the jack pines north of the farm and out into the prairie as he neared Winnipeg.

In Winnipeg, looking and feeling out of place in the hall full of Canadian lawyers dressed in their tweed sport coats and three-piece suits, Raven waited until Angela began speaking before entering the rear of the hall. Their eyes met momentarily during a pause in her introductory remarks. The pause continued as their gazes locked, which caused a few heads in the audience to swivel around to see what was holding her attention.

Raven was impressed by her composure during the questions that followed the formal speech and by her conviction of the justness of the RICO Act, which affords a civil remedy for persons victimized by racketeer-influenced activity.

It's too bad the criminal procedures are so ineffective against the organized crime families, he thought. *RICO doesn't do someone like Kari much good.*

At the end of the lecture, Raven waited as Angela discussed her speech with various lawyers who came forward. She obviously enjoyed the intellectual stimulation of the discussion. He admired the poise of this gifted and attractive woman. Finally, she broke free and approached him.

"You certainly do stand out in a crowd," she remarked. "I thought I was going to lose it when you walked into the hall even though I was expecting you."

Their eyes met as their hands clasped. Immediately they felt a surge of electricity, and Angela dropped her eyes to look at the powerful, tanned hands holding hers. They felt alone in the room, even amid scores of Canadian lawyers.

How could I feel so assured before this crowd of lawyers a moment ago, and now feel like this—just by touching his hands? Angela looked up at Raven.

"Are you ready to get out of here?" he asked.

"Yes, I am," she said, thinking she sounded a bit breathless and pondering the implications of what she was getting into.

On the way back to his farm, Raven talked about the experimental crops he'd introduced to their fields, told her about the animals on the place, and described his farming partnership with Lorne.

Angela just focused on Raven, wondering how such an intelligent man could live essentially alone in such a tiny community without marrying. As they entered the Ravendal land, Raven's bay gelding and the Appaloosa raced along the pasture fence parallel to the vehicle. The pet ravens swooped ahead of the car.

"What gorgeous horses!" exclaimed Angela. "Is the big one yours?"

"Yes."

"Then if we go riding, do I get to ride the pretty, spotted horse?"

"I think that would be a good idea." Raven remained silent about his feelings for the Appaloosa. "She's gentle, and she's used to being handled by a woman."

Angela wondered what was behind that remark but chose not to ask.

As they parked the truck in the yard, Angela looked about and marveled at the fresh beauty of the place. A flight of wood ducks passed low overhead, setting their wings as they dropped into one of the ponds about a block from the house. "It's so peaceful here. I can understand why you love it."

"That's the way it makes me feel . . . at peace. And I feel particularly good knowing that while I make a living here, the place is also home for so many wild creatures. Shall I show you the house?"

As he took Angela's hand and led her up the kitchen steps, a surge of energy passed between them.

As they entered the kitchen, in the old log part of the house, Angela felt herself trembling slightly. She touched Raven's arm. "Raven, do you have any idea what I'm feeling?" she murmured.

He turned to her. Before they knew it, they were in each other's arms. A fierce, sweet desire overcame them as their bodies embraced. It was a time of total turmoil and confusion, as their mouths found each other. For both of these strong, independent people, it was a completely novel experience.

As they parted momentarily, Angela murmured, "God, how I want you."

It was all the prompting either of them needed. Raven and Angela somehow floated through the house to his bedroom, undressing one another and leaving a trail of clothing as they went. Their lovemaking was wild with complete abandon as they released themselves to the powerful emotions surging through them. They felt themselves swirling ever higher, and around and around, as they lost themselves in each other's bodies, their senses becoming almost excruciatingly intense until they reached a peak of ecstasy and tumbled down into each other's arms.

As Angela lay in Raven's arms, they both began chuckling. "My God," she finally said, "did you have any idea?"

"Who could have any idea it would be anything like this? I think we might be a little dangerous together. I'd hate to be caught between us when all that energy gets released."

Thinking about the trail of shoes and clothing, they both began laughing again.

Later, still lying in bed, enjoying being close and talking, Angela noticed that the bandage on Raven's shoulder had come loose, and she saw the deep, reddish-brown scar running along his shoulder. "What happened?"

"You have to be careful when you're crawling around under hot, running tractors."

"You really burned yourself."

"Yes, I did," he replied.

The rest of the day was a wonderful idyll for Angela. Raven saddled up the horses and took her for a tour of the entire farm. Finally, they rode through the woods to Lorne and Beverly's place. As they rode into the yard, Little Lars cried out, "She's riding Kari's horse!"

"Who's Kari?" asked Angela.

"My niece, his sister."

Then they were met by Lorne and Beverly and caught up in a flurry of greetings and explanations. Raven was beaming when he saw how warmly Lorne and Beverly welcomed Angela to their home. Poised and assured, Angela launched into a discussion with Lorne and Beverly about the farming operation and the economy and explained how different her background was from theirs. Little Lars remained a bit more skeptical of Angela but eventually, with smiles and encouragement, she won him over. Lorne and Beverly noted the glow on the faces of Angela and Raven and smiled at one another.

After a light supper, Raven and Angela mounted up again and rode back to his house.

Later, as they drove off the farm, heading back toward the university, Angela said, "Raven, I love it here. When can I come again?"

Raven smiled. "Soon, I hope. You're always welcome."

They drove on in silence for a time, each lost in thought. Finally, Raven broke the silence. "Kari and I raised and trained the Appaloosa from a colt. We loved riding our horses around the farm. Then she went away to college. She got tricked and forced into sex bondage by evil people. When she tried to escape and come home, they murdered her. It's the worst thing that ever happened to our family." Raven had told the heartbreaking tale as if in a trance. Then a torrent of tears poured from his eyes, and he pulled over to the shoulder, where he sat shaking with emotion for several long minutes. Finally, he pulled back onto the highway, and they drove on again in silence.

17

THE NEXT MORNING, WITH A SIGH, Flash Maruska
draped his massive bulk over a chair in Henry
Grogan's office.

"How ya doing, Flash?"

"Not so good. Rosalee's got us on short rations again. She's
a little ticked about the weight I've been gaining lately."

Henry never ceased to be amused with Flash's huge weight
swings. "You mean just because you ordered out for three pizzas the other day Rosalee thinks you've been gaining weight?"

"Well, I have gained an ounce or two."

"How much?"

Flash rolled his eyes. "Nineteen pounds!"

"Imagine, a guy gains a mere nineteen pounds and the
next thing you know his wife won't cook for him," said Henry
in mock sympathy. "Which diet you on now?"

"This time, Rosalee's gone scientific," said Flash, producing
a glossy, circular plastic set of concentric dials. "See, Henry?"
he said. "You can set the inside depending on your height
and weight. Then you adjust the next dial based on activity,
for calories consumed. Then, the outside is the amount of

calories you can have per day. So you divide the calories you can have per day by the number of meals you plan to eat. Then you take this little book here and figure out the calories for each size portion of each thing you eat," he said, producing a small calorie-counter book.

"How's it going so far?"

"I've been on it for three days, since the start of the weekend." Flash sighed. "It's awful. I'm hungry all the time." Relief spread over his face as he remembered why he'd come into Henry's office. He was grateful for the opportunity to change the subject. "I've been thinking about the start of this whole situation in the families," he said, referring to the war that had been raging for weeks.

"So?"

"It might be just a hunch, but just on the chance there was only one shooter on the Ronnie and Vito Cerrillo hits and maybe only one involved in the Gambucci raid, I've been thinking it might not be too dumb to run some kind of an analysis of recent victims who have a reason to go after the Cerrillos, and maybe the Gambuccis. Do you know of anyone who could put together a little study for me?"

Henry pondered Flash's request. "Well, I think you're betting on a real long shot. But I could ask my friend Joyce over at the governor's strike force to see what she can come up with. I mean, she seems to love doing surveys."

"I'd appreciate it. It may be nothing. On the other hand, I couldn't sleep last night—my stomach was growling so much—so I got up and prowled around the house. Some of my best results have come to me during those midnight prowls when I'm dieting. Right now, it's just a feeling, but I'm wondering if there isn't one guy out there so pissed off at the Mob that he's gotten inspired to solo action."

"OK, OK, I know all about your famous hunches. Once in a blue moon, they pay off. I'll see what I can do."

18

May 1977

FOR SOME TIME, GUNAR RAVENDAL HAD BEEN thinking about his cousin Carl's mangled hand. When he thought about mobsters trailing Carl's children to and from school as part of terroristic threats aimed at extortion from Carl's family business, he began to draw again on the great, implacable rage lying deep within him. Over the past several weeks, he had concentrated on the microfilms of the old Los Angeles newspapers and the organized crime strike force charts and studies of the Mafia in California. Again, the strike force studies had proven particularly helpful, pinpointing the legitimate banking and illegitimate extortion activities in the Los Angeles area. Raven was fairly certain of his targets.

The families involved in terrorizing Carl certainly had to be headed by Thomas "Tito" Francone. Tito was a poster boy for the "modern" mafioso. Forever protesting his innocence and contributing to various charities, Tito was frequently found in the company of various movie stars, Las Vegas entertainers, and other prominent personalities. Ever the ladies' man, it was rumored that Tito supplied women for many politicians and businessmen. He lived in Beverly Hills and officed in a beautiful building owned by the family near Marina del Rey. Tito took great pride in the wall of his office that was completely covered with autographed photographs of him with various movie stars, politicians on both the state and national levels, and other celebrities.

Two decades of total insulation from the violent activities of his underlings had made him sublimely confident. Seldom did Tito ever take a direct hand in such distasteful activities as holding the fingers of some poor sap like Carl in a car door. For several years now, all he had to do was suggest that something ought to be done about a stubborn businessman or politician, and the job got done. In the case of Carl Johnson, Tito had attended a board of directors meeting for the bank involved, had learned of Carl's stubbornness, and had simply told Nate Gottlieb, president of the bank and longtime "accountant" for the Francone family, to arrange for application of the muscle needed to take over Johnson Import-Export Company.

Gottlieb told him that it seemed like a logical task for the Barberas, and Tito agreed. Nate then arranged for a brief meeting with Jackie Barbera, head of enforcement for Francone activities on the waterfront. Jackie, in turn, delegated the actual dirty work to his younger brother, Wally. The sadistic Wally Barbera, anxious to make a reputation with the family, had personally seen to both the mangling of Carl Johnson's fingers and the telephone threats that had brought the Johnson business into partnership with Francone's.

Raven didn't know the specifics of the violent physical and mental attack upon Carl Johnson. However, he was certain the chain of command behind it had come from Tito Francone, via Nate Gottlieb or someone else at the bank. Planning his trip, he decided the basic format followed in the Gambucci raid was better than attempting to "borrow" a vehicle, as he had when he'd made the attack on the Cerrillos. Because of the wide-open, mobile situation in Southern California, he was uncertain of what to bring along in the way of weaponry.

To cover various possibilities, he packed his rifles in the suit carrier and briefcase and also added the sawed-off shotgun in the toolbox. In addition, he decided to take his long-barreled Colt .357 Magnum, which he'd owned ever since he began his Alaskan trips. Designed to stop a Kodiak or grizzly bear encountered at close range in the bush, the weapon had awesome shocking power. Raven had never fired it except in practice, but he had read that it could penetrate an automobile from the rear, plow through both seats and instrument panel, and still make it into the engine block, stopping the vehicle. It seemed sufficient for any close-in work that might present itself.

Following his packing, he spent the remainder of the evening studying his *Official Airline Guide* and a map of the greater Los Angeles area. The following morning, he drove again to the Grand Forks airport. Leaving the Ramcharger in the lot, he purchased a ticket to Denver in his own name. Arriving in Denver three hours later, he picked up his luggage at the carousel and headed for the Western Airlines desk. There, using cash, he bought a ticket to San Diego in the name of Clyde James.

Once again, no problems had arisen during the process of checking the suitcase with toolbox containing the parts of the sawed-off shotgun and pistol. Nor had there been any difficulty getting the garment bag and briefcase with their concealed weaponry through the airport monitors. Once in San Diego, Raven debated over whether or not he should use his Pennsylvania driver's license again. Deciding that it might draw too much attention, he checked his luggage into an airport locker and took a cab down to Old Town San Diego.

There, he walked among the old Spanish-era buildings, looking for an opportunity. Finding none, he headed to a waterfront shopping and dining complex. Amid the retro atmosphere of nineteenth-century California, he wandered through the shops, mingling with the tourists and locals. Although he made several vigils in the bars and restaurants of the area, he didn't find an opportunity to relieve someone of his ID, as he'd been able to do with the drunk laborer in Philadelphia.

Finally, Raven wandered over to the Cabrillo National Monument. Loitering about the area, he watched two men flirting. One of the pair was rather obviously not yet out of the closet. Middle-aged, tall, and dressed in a business suit, he was quite ill at ease as he struck up a conversation with a tanned, bleached-blond young man in tight blue jeans and net muscle shirt. The businessman was approximately the same age and height as Raven. He wore rose-tinted glasses and kept nervously running his fingers through his dark hair as he chatted with his intended new friend. Soon they strolled off together.

Raven trailed them at a distance and observed them heading into a restaurant-bar that was heavy on a nautical atmosphere—including hanging fishing nets, glass buoys, and aquariums full of tropical fish. Taking a position near the end of the bar, he ordered a beer and continued observing the romance unfolding before him. After a couple of drinks, the businessman became increasingly more casual, draping his suit coat over the back of his chair and loosening his tie. After another round of drinks, the conversation became more intimate and animated as the participants began gently touching each other's wrists and knees.

Finally, the couple arose from their drinks and headed into the men's room. Looking quickly about, Raven walked by their table, reached into his pocket, and "accidentally" dropped his keys. Kneeling next to the businessman's chair to pick them up, he quickly reached into the breast pocket of the suit coat and extracted a billfold. Fearing that he might be observed, he picked up the keys, glancing about. No one had observed him. Shoving the billfold into his pocket, he strolled back to his seat at the bar. Opening it, he found a driver's license, credit cards, and, to his surprise, photographs of the man with his wife and children.

He removed the driver's license and one of the gasoline credit cards. Then, looking about the darkened bar again, he walked by the table and quickly replaced the billfold in the breast pocket of the suit coat. He then proceeded into the men's room, entering it just as the businessman and his new friend emerged. Obviously entranced with one another, they paid no attention to Raven. A few minutes later, Raven strolled out of the men's room and saw the happy couple ordering another round of drinks. He left the restaurant, speculating about the fate of the businessman and his family.

Within half an hour, he'd rented a car and was headed up Interstate 5 into Los Angeles. Once there, he switched onto the 405 and followed it past the Marina del Rey exit to Culver City. There, he checked into a motel, paying cash in advance for three nights' lodging. He pulled out the telephone directory and looked up the location of the bank that had taken over his cousin Carl's business. He located it in Inglewood, not far from the Hollywood Park Racetrack.

Having done this, Raven got back into the car and drove to Beverly Hills. Finding a local telephone directory in a phone booth, he was amazed to find a listing and address for Tito Francone. *Apparently, Francone feels so legitimate that he acts like an ordinary citizen*, he mused. Getting back into the car, he cruised through Beverly Hills until he found the Francone address. An imposing, Moorish-style home sat seventy-five yards back from the street amid towering palm trees and behind a wrought iron fence. The fence bore small signs from a security company every thirty feet. The house itself appeared impregnable.

After making his observations of the house, Raven drove back to a drive-in restaurant on Santa Monica Boulevard, picked up two bacon and tomato cheeseburgers, french fries, and two Styrofoam containers of coffee. Then he headed back to the Francone residence and parked approximately one half block away. Yet another vigil began.

After waiting nearly two hours, Raven saw the wrought iron gates slowly swing open, operating on a signal tripped from somewhere in the house. Seconds later, a silver Porsche Targa pulled through the gates, turned left, and headed directly toward Raven's car. Turning his face downward, he caught a glimpse of the occupants as the car flashed by.

To his amazement, he saw Tito Francone behind the wheel, accompanied by a famous, ash-blonde vocalist who was still immensely popular with middle-aged Americans even though she was nearing the end of her career. Unaccustomed to seeing celebrities at close range, he caught his breath. After a few seconds, his composure returned. He started the engine, checked for police, and then turned the car into a tight U-turn and began following the Porsche.

Somehow the sight of the famous singer troubled Raven. It seemed improper to be stalking the companion of such a beloved icon of American music. Angrily, he shook off his feelings, muttering to himself, "Just because the devil manages to have some respectable companions doesn't make him any different inside. Wealth and fame tend to get people elevated to respectability without any analysis of whether or not they deserve it."

He continued trailing the Porsche out of Beverly Hills, along Santa Monica Boulevard to the Pacific Coast Highway, and then past the J. Paul Getty Museum to Malibu. From there, the car turned up Malibu Canyon Road. Eventually, it turned off in a private driveway. Raven continued past the driveway for about half a mile, where he made a U-turn. He returned and finally found a place to park on the shoulder about a block from the driveway. He resumed his vigil, sipping black coffee and munching on the second burger, both of which were now cold.

Suddenly, it dawned on him that surprise was of the essence. An immediate strike was probably as good as one carefully planned after days of careful stalking. Reaching into the back seat, he opened his suitcase and removed the sawed-off shotgun and .357 Magnum. Both were fully loaded. Raven placed both weapons on the seat beside him. Then he rolled down the front windows and waited, listening.

After about forty-five minutes, he heard the throaty roar of the Porsche's engine as it descended the hilly driveway. It immediately turned back down Malibu Canyon Road, moving fast. Raven began following the Porsche with his headlights off, but as the Porsche drew away, being driven expertly by Tito Francone, he realized the futility of catching it with lights off. As the Porsche rounded a curve, he turned the headlights back on and stepped on the accelerator. Closing the gap between the rental car and the Porsche was difficult; Raven had no success until both vehicles turned onto the freeway just outside Malibu. As they turned east along Santa Monica Bay, Raven pushed the rental car to the limit and began gaining on the Porsche. After about a mile at speeds close to eighty miles per hour, he pulled close behind the Porsche.

Several times he saw Tito Francone's eyes watching him in the rearview mirror. Convinced Francone had seen his face, Raven decided he had nothing to lose. Holding the steering wheel in his left hand, he flipped the safety off the sawed-off shotgun with his right hand and floored the accelerator. The car quickly pulled abreast Francone's Porsche. As the cars pulled even, he heard Francone shouting obscenities. "Motherfucker, what you doin' following me?"

As Raven pulled the shotgun above the level of the door, Francone's eyes widened. Just before Tito could dive into the seat, Raven squeezed the trigger. The blast ripped into Francone's face, instantly transforming it into a crimson mask of blood as all the facial tissues gave way. Francone's car screamed out of control, left the highway, hit the foot of the ditch, and began cartwheeling, end over end. Raven saw the body sail in an arc through the air like a rag doll, flying for over fifty feet, where it fell motionless on the sand. Immediately, cars going the opposite direction began to hit their brakes. No cars were visible behind Raven, and he sped down the highway, concealing the shotgun on the floor beneath the front passenger seat and the .357 Magnum beneath the driver's seat as he drove.

Raven had no illusions about the extent of the police activity that would shortly ensue, so as soon as he reached Santa Monica, he pulled off the road and put the weapons back into the toolbox, which he set in the bottom of his suitcase. He immediately headed onto Interstate 10 and then back to Interstate 405 and south to Los Angeles International Airport. Leaving the rental car in the long-term parking ramp, he walked swiftly to the Western Airlines ticket counter, where he purchased a commuter ticket in the name of Richard Archer to San Francisco.

An hour later in San Francisco, he used cash to buy another ticket to Denver in the name of Gerald Olsen. Arriving in Denver too late for the last flight to Grand Forks, he took a shuttle bus to an airport hotel, checked in, and ordered beer from room service. After the beer arrived, he sank back on the bed, turning on the television to see if the late news had any coverage of the shooting.

As he sipped the beer, he realized that all his nerve endings were tingling and it was likely that he'd have great difficulty sleeping. He tried to will himself to sleep by thinking of the farm and then of Alaska and the Northwest Territories. But the bloody face of Tito Francone kept coming to mind. Finally, he gave up. As he stared at the ceiling, he thought about Angela and how she'd probably hate him if she knew what he'd done. Tears welled up in his eyes as he considered the berserker he'd become and the man he'd been before becoming intent on revenge.

Raven spent the night in turmoil, his nerves rubbed raw by the conflicts raging within him. He'd exacted enough vengeance to satisfy his emotional need to strike out after the loss of Kari. But he still felt driven to act—by his implacable hatred of an organization bent on preying on the innocents of society, by the pitiful inability of the legal process to deal with it, and by ancient warrior instinct to keep battling, against all odds, until either you or the enemy is vanquished. And then, he acknowledged, there was another powerful impulse fighting for dominance—his need for Angela.

19

S IX HOURS LATER, AT ONE O'CLOCK on a Saturday afternoon, Raven stood in the hallway of an apartment
building on the outskirts of Grand Forks, North
Dakota, rapping on the door of an apartment three blocks
from the university. Angela, clad in white silk lounging paja-
mas, was grading papers. Annoyed at the intrusion of the
knock, she opened the door with a frown on her face. Then,
as recognition dawned, her mouth dropped open, and a shiver
of excitement went through her.

"My God," she stammered. "I thought it was one of my
students."

Raven stood silently looking at her. Then their eyes met,
and for the first time, Angela saw hurt, longing, and vulnera-
bility in his eyes. In an instant they were in each other's arms,
tenderly yielding to their desires.

"Raven, each time I see you, it's new—as though I'm
meeting you for the first time, again and again."

"Don't talk, Angela. We can talk later," said Raven, gently
lifting her in his arms and carrying her off to the bedroom.
This time, the loving was as gentle and caring as their earlier

contact had been fierce and demanding. Waves of sweetness swept over them, ebbing and flowing, gently lifting them up and letting them down. At the peak, they both felt a surge of ecstasy, mingled with a bittersweet wonderment over whether another moment, never again to be duplicated, had been reached. Then, entwined in Angela's arms, Raven slept the deepest of sleeps. Listening to his breathing, Angela gently stroked his brow and ran her fingers over his shoulders and neck, tracing the scar on his shoulder, allowing her mind to float, happy to be focused on nothing but the sleeping giant sprawled in her arms.

Four hours later, Raven awoke in the twilight to find Angela standing naked before him. Immediately, they were in each other's arms again, exploring one another's bodies, prolonging the experience, giving and taking pleasure. Lips and tongues running over bodies, both seeking to delay and prolong . . . and then, as the futility of curbing their appetites became apparent, giving way to wild abandon. They were laughing and rolling, almost childlike, as their passions again ran away with them and they found themselves transported ever upward to an ultimate peak of ecstasy and then back down to that best of all times when two lovers, having totally abandoned themselves to one another, discover they're both lovers and best friends, able to confide in each other with complete trust.

"How did you ever get involved in criminal law?" Raven asked. "I mean, someone as lovely as you in that dark world?"

"You really want to know?"

"Are you afraid I'll ask something you don't want to tell me?"

"No. I want you to know everything about me. I just don't want to tell you anything bad or sad. Seems like you need to hear nothing but happy things right now."

"I need to know as much as I can about you. How did it happen?"

Taking a deep breath, Angela looked over his shoulder into the twilight. "I'll tell it to you like a story. Maybe then it will be easier. Once there was a little girl, living in a little town on Long Island. Many people thought she was Italian. They didn't understand that there isn't just one kind of Italian. Most of her friends saw no difference between Sicilians and Italians. But to the little girl's mother's family, there was a big difference. You see, the little girl's mother was from an Italian family with money and respect, both in Italy and America. But the little girl's father was 'Sichy' or Siciliano, which was a nasty word to the little girl's mother, aunts, uncles, and cousins. But her mother had fallen in love with this young Sichy prizefighter, and her family never let them forget that Sicilians were a 'lesser species' of Italian. Although they invited them to their family gatherings and gave her money and helped them buy a house, they never let them forget that the gifts and the hospitality were for their daughter, not for a Sichy tough guy.

"Then, mismanaged by his corrupt owners, the prizefighter was matched to an opponent far beyond his ability, and he lost. It was no accident that his manager and friends made a lot of money betting on the fight. Then they told the

Sichy prizefighter that if he wanted his beautiful Italian wife and little girl to stay safe, he'd better help them collect debts. The fighter felt he had no choice. He began collecting debts on the Island, in Brooklyn and Queens, and on the docks. He was good at his job. Eventually, money flowed in.

"Then one day, an idealistic district attorney began a crusade against the mobsters that were running him. The boss's son, groomed for leadership, was indicted for manslaughter. Then, the capo of all the capos called in the young fighter and made him an offer he couldn't refuse. He had a choice: face the consequences of not cooperating, or confess to the manslaughter charges brought against the don's son. If he confessed, he was guaranteed monthly deposits in his checking account that would radically improve the standard of living of his wife and daughter. In addition, he was promised a release from service and a fully stocked Italian restaurant to be run as a legitimate business for the rest of his life.

"The only hobbies of the young Sicilian were wine-making and cooking. He shared these hobbies with his daughter. They worked together, standing under his Franklin Delano Roosevelt posters and American flags in the basement and next to wine barrels in his kitchen. These were really the only two rooms in the house where he felt at home. So, he confided his plan to his daughter and wife and went to prison. The daughter practiced her Italian cooking all during his stay in prison. Seven years later, with time off for good behavior, she and her father looked forward to his coming release the next month.

"But it turned out the dream of a post-incarceration restaurant was an empty one. Two weeks before his release date, the don's son's men approached him in the prison yard as he exercised. Three men approached him—two held his arms as a third plunged a shiv into his heart. The don's son was now in control of the family. He didn't want anyone outside of his immediate family who could ever testify against him. Of course, out of respect for women and children, the payments continued. But the dream shared by the little girl and her father was never to be."

Raven ached to hold Angela as he watched the tears wash down her cheeks. Finally, she spoke again. "Now do you understand why a nice Italian girl would go into criminal law and join the Manhattan prosecutor's office?"

"What can be done?" he asked. "And what made you stop prosecuting and go into teaching?"

"Frustration. Contract judges. Insulated gang bosses. In a word, I guess, corruption. Maybe, before the latest spread of cocaine, crack, and marijuana—and all the money they bring to paid-off cops, prosecutors, and judges—there was reason for hope in the law-enforcement process. I think that now the only answer is in education. Maybe someday the public at large will wake up and smell the coffee. If it isn't too late by then."

"What about now? What about the victims? Who speaks for them?"

"I'm afraid nobody at present. This is getting a little heavy. Anyway, I haven't seen any mafiosi in North Dakota or northern Minnesota," she said, hoping to lighten up the conversation. "Just hold me. We're talking a little too much," she said, smiling tenderly. They sat for a while, staring into the twilight, each lost in thought.

Then Angela sprang up. "It just dawned on me. I've never cooked for you! Do you like Italian food?"

"Love it!"

The remainder of the evening was spent laughing and joking in Angela's kitchen as the seductive fragrances of veal Marsala, Italian bread, and a wonderful salad with homemade Italian dressing filled the kitchen.

Later that night, driving home, Raven pondered Angela's statements about how drug money was corrupting the legal process throughout America. He kept recalling classic movies that centered on Prohibition-era stories, another instance in which a widely desired illegal substance created conflict. In fact, from everything he'd read, the origins of the Mob in America were directly connected to Prohibition. As he considered the situation, a plan was forming in his mind.

20

THE FOLLOWING WEEK, PRESS COVERAGE of the shooting of Tito Francone gave further credence to Angela's statements and spurred Raven further into his plan. News headlines had been full of eulogies for Tito from the lips of his show business and politician friends. Other news stories about his association with banking interests rumored to be connected with drug money in California, Nevada, New York, Chicago, and especially Florida also ran. From his research, Raven knew that bankers for the Mob in New York had embraced Las Vegas as a "free zone" for the investment and laundering of their illegal money.

Connections among Mafia families from the Midwest, Florida, and California had arisen. When certain Jewish mobsters had been run out of Minneapolis and St. Paul, for example, they took refuge in Florida. Many families were currently involved in banking and laundering of drug money in a big way. The demand for drugs and drug money in California, New York, and Chicago had further cemented the ties. Thus, the Cerrillos enjoyed a nationwide network built on the apparently limitless market for drugs in New York and Los Angeles, the consequent huge amounts of money being made in Florida, and the need for the laundering of this money in Miami, Las Vegas, and California.

The traditional ties between illegal booze, untaxed cigarettes, and typical New York drug money had accelerated exponentially with the advent of crack and the huge new markets and profits it brought. Where Raven had been in a quandary over who his targets should be in order to spread the war into the Florida scene, he now had a new focus. The Gambuccis and other families had attempted to grow to nationwide status, but the Gottliebs led transplanted midwestern mobsters to "banking" in Florida, Vegas, and California. The other families had forced them to primarily consort with the wilder "new" Cuban and Colombian families. Warfare between the two groups in Florida could easily spread, with proper encouragement, to the West Coast, Chicago, and Las Vegas.

The perfect target was Isadore "Babe" Levinson, now known as Shelby Bloom, formerly of Minneapolis—now, infinitely wealthier, of Miami and Palm Beach. Owner of hotels, savings and loans, and banks all along the southeast coast of Florida, Bloom's empire was so great that he enjoyed great favor among all but the oldest Anglo money in south Florida.

Huddled in their enclaves in and around Palm Beach, these powerful retirees from legitimate American business did their best to ignore the chaos that was rampant around them. Ensconced in their closed communities, with guarded gates and increasingly sophisticated security systems, these former citizens of the great cities of America with their astonishing wealth could perhaps have done something about the mess that spread all over southeast Florida. But they no longer had the will to fight. Their battles were primarily with their brokers, who were back in New York, Detroit, Cleveland, Chicago, Minneapolis, Boston, or Toronto.

A week after his visit to Angela's apartment, Raven flew from Grand Forks to Minneapolis, where he purchased a bargain excursion fare to Naples, Florida. There, using his Pennsylvania driver's license, he rented a car and headed east on US Highway 41, also known as Alligator Alley, to Miami. At the legal speed limit, the drive took three hours. About an hour after he arrived in Miami, he strolled into the lobby of a lavish hotel that towered above Collins Avenue, headquarters for Shelby Bloom. He checked in under the name P. V. Silvano, the initial and last name of his Pennsylvania driver's license, giving as his address the correct street but wrong street number from the license. In his room, he assembled the Ruger 10/22, complete with cylinder full of cartridges, and attached its scope. Stuffing the weapon from corner to corner in the bottom of a long tennis bag, he covered it with a beach towel, warm-up suit, and tennis racket, the handle of which he left protruding from the end of the bag. He then donned tennis shorts, shirt, sandals, sunglasses, and beach hat and descended to the lobby. There he lounged for a while, attempting to learn the where-abouts of Bloom's offices. Sipping an iced tea in the lobby, he overheard several businesspeople asking the desk clerk where

Mr. Bloom's offices were located. Eventually, he pinpointed Bloom's office, halfway down a hallway off the lobby, behind a thick glass door. Glancing up, he observed closed-circuit cameras scanning the lobby, the glass doorway, and the hallway. In addition, a guard sat outside the office doorway, reading the *Miami Herald*. It was apparent that security was prohibitively strong in the office area.

Raven strolled out of the lobby and down to the tennis cabana. The pro was out giving a lesson, and Raven availed himself of the opportunity to check the schedules. From his studies, he learned that Bloom didn't use the hotel tennis courts—though Raven knew Bloom was an avid tennis buff who sponsored various tournaments in the Miami area and backed young pros from time to time. Next, he surveyed the parking lot for armored limousines. Again, nothing useful. But eventually, by overhearing service staff, he learned Bloom's vehicle was one of the few kept in underground parking beneath the hotel. Totally frustrated, he spent the remainder of the day and evening lounging around the hotel, attempting to get a fix on Bloom, to no avail.

At eleven o'clock, he finally headed for his room, searching his mind for an opening. Just before he drifted off to sleep, he recalled an old newspaper article about Bloom. Actually, it wasn't about him at all. It was a feature about a famous old Miami Beach restaurant renowned for its stone crabs. Raven recalled a photograph of Bloom and the proprietor, along with a discussion of how the ordinary public must wait for hours for the famous stone crabs, whereas a favored few, out of long association with the owner, were afforded immediate entry. Bloom, if Raven remembered right, was a regular Friday evening visitor when the crabs were in season.

The next morning, Thursday, Raven drove immediately to the south point of Miami Beach where the restaurant was located and surveyed the area. Across the street, several blocks had been razed. Piles of rubble were scattered across a vacant area covering several blocks. Caterpillar tracks and paths for heavy earthmoving equipment crisscrossed the area. About a block from the restaurant, the land rose into a small ridge from which he had a good view of the side and front doors of the restaurant.

Returning late that afternoon, Raven found that the formal parking immediately across the street gave way to some informal parking in the construction area. Pulling his car into the rise, he determined that the sight lines to the restaurant's door were excellent and there'd be sufficient early-evening light for his rifle scope. His greatest concern was the problem of getting off Miami Beach. There were only four options available: MacArthur Causeway, Julia Tuttle Causeway, Collins Avenue north to John F. Kennedy Memorial Causeway, or all the way north on Collins Avenue to North Miami. The location of Miami International Airport, far to the west, gave him great concern.

He spent the rest of the night exploring different escape routes and the side streets on Miami Beach itself. As he turned in for the night, Raven was uncertain if he should take the risk of a shot from the southern tip of Miami Beach, given the distinct possibility that the Miami police, if alerted early enough, could effectively bottle up the entire island within minutes. At midnight, he returned to his room, where he lay on the bed, paying little attention to the television as he pondered the risks and problems of the next day. Just before he drifted off to sleep around one o'clock, he hit upon a plan. The discipline to reject the instinct to flee after an attack would be the hardest part.

21

THE NEXT MORNING, RAVEN PAID CASH in advance for another night's lodging. Then, dressed again in tennis clothes and carrying his tennis bag, he walked northward along Collins Avenue, passing several hotels until he found one that rented the old, balloon-tired bicycles available for rent throughout south Florida. Watching the young Cuban attendant for a while, he noted that he was doing a brisk trade in the bicycles and that he accepted reservations of room numbers from the guests without checking their keys.

Fifteen minutes later, giving the name of Thomas Welch, he checked out a bicycle and pedaled it southward along Miami Beach. Eventually, he made his way down to the public beach at the south end of the island. The empty lot where a proud old hotel had once stood lay between the beach and Collins Avenue. To the south was the construction area he'd surveyed the day before. Strolling southward along the ocean, he wheeled the bicycle along the path under the palm trees that had formerly fronted the old hotel. No longer popular, the beach was nearly deserted except for some small boys fishing off a jetty at the end and a few surf casters scattered along South Beach.

Spreading his beach towel on the sand, Raven stretched out and surveyed the scene. After observing the locale for about an hour, he gathered his belongings, put them in the basket of the bicycle, and pedaled past the restaurant. As he'd feared the day before, the streets were congested with delivery trucks and other traffic. The neighborhood was a curious blend of deserted warehouses, homes of Cubans and geriatric Miami Beach regulars, and a few new houses, giving evidence of the beginning of a gentrification of the area. At times, a flurry of traffic filled the streets to such a degree that any rapid exit by car would prove impossible.

Having surveyed the entire scene, Raven returned to the hotel, where he ate a lunch of lobster salad, fruit, and iced tea. After lunch, he returned to his room and forced himself to lie down for an hour. Unable to sleep, he willed his muscles to relax, group by group, beginning from his toes and working up through his legs, arms, trunk, and entire body. Finally, he snoozed for a half hour, charging his energy for the evening.

In the late afternoon, Raven took the garment bag and briefcase with him down to his car and locked them in the trunk. Then he returned to the hotel with his tennis bag, reclaimed his bicycle, and rode it down to the tip of Miami Beach again, where he resumed his vigil until just before dusk.

Setting his beach towel and bag in the basket of the bicycle, he rode slowly in the general direction of the restaurant. Already, a small number of patrons stood outside the door awaiting entry. Raven pushed the bicycle to the foot of a construction sign near the crest of the knoll and strolled to the top of the rise, carrying the tennis bag. Acting nonchalant, he spread the beach towel out on the far side of the knoll and lay on his stomach, peering over the beach bag at the restaurant.

Opposite the restaurant, next to some deserted buildings, two derelicts shared a bottle hidden in a paper bag. No one paid them any mind. The neighborhood was at the precarious point where it would either submit to gentrification or succumb to total decay. Seafood trucks and other food-service vehicles rumbled up to the alleyway beside the restaurant, unloading food for the evening trade. Just before dark, Raven reached into the tennis bag and removed the 10/22. He placed the barrel along the ground, just to the left of the tennis bag. The shadow of the construction sign fell across him as he'd anticipated, and he was certain that he was virtually unseen from the street. The light-gathering scope collected light from the setting sun, brightly illuminating the front and side of the restaurant. Through the scope, Raven was able to distinguish facial characteristics of the patrons lined up on the sidewalk, awaiting entry.

As he waited, Raven wondered if the good luck that had enabled him to make a swift strike on Tito Francone would last. He wondered if the newspaper account he'd read about Bloom's Friday-night devotion to the restaurant was an exaggeration. He knew from his eavesdropping in the lobby that Bloom was in town. He didn't know what kind of car Bloom used or what personal protection he normally took with him in the evening.

At dusk, a white Cadillac limousine slid up to the curb in front of the restaurant. A chauffeur-bodyguard immediately walked to the restaurant and spoke briefly with the doorman. After a moment's conversation, the chauffeur moved to open the limousine's rear passenger-side door. Two women, one in her thirties, the other in her sixties, emerged. Raven assumed they were Bloom's wife and daughter. The chauffeur then hurried to open the driver's-side rear door. Raven peered through the scope at the small, bent figure who emerged, elegantly dressed in a cream-colored tropical suit that contrasted with the deeply creased, tanned face and curly, steel-gray hair of Shelby Bloom.

Confident of his marksmanship, Raven opted again for a head shot. As the fabulously wealthy launderer of drug money stepped onto the sidewalk on the arm of his chauffeur, Raven squeezed off one round. Without the silencer, which he had removed for greater accuracy, the sharp crack of the rifle sounded, and Bloom threw up his hands as the bullet crashed through the rear of his skull and mushroomed into his brain. His arms flew outward and flailed about. He began to fall, spread-eagle, backward. The chauffeur caught Bloom as he fell and immediately reached into his jacket for his shoulder holster. A second shot from Raven blew out the chauffeur's left eye, traveling into his brain and exploding against the right side of his skull. As the chauffeur sank on top of Bloom, the women began to scream. Several tourists began to shout.

Raven seized the moment of panic to thrust the Ruger into the tennis bag, which he jammed into the basket of the bicycle. He pedaled swiftly across the rough ground, heading for the sidewalk in front of the razed hotel. Once there, he pumped furiously, speeding by elderly couples out for their evening strolls, drawing some curious glances. Forcing himself to slow down to a more moderate speed, he proceeded along the sidewalk for another half block and then turned left for a block, where he hit Collins Avenue. As he headed north on Collins, he heard sirens approaching from the west and north. Turning left on the first side street, he entered an area of smaller, older hotels interspersed with new condominium developments. Turning north again, he continued parallel to Collins Avenue. He heard at least five sirens as police cars raced to the restaurant.

Five minutes later, he'd gone farther north than the bicycle rental location. Turning right, he rode back to Collins Avenue, and rode back to return the bicycle. He was relieved to find a new attendant, about the same age as the other.

Raven walked swiftly back to the parking lot of his hotel. Opening the trunk of his rental car, he set the tennis bag in it and took out a navy jogging suit. After he pulled it over his tennis clothes, he felt much less conspicuous. As he walked up the steps of the hotel, it was apparent that his initial suspicions about escaping Miami Beach had been correct. From the front steps of the hotel, he could hear the sirens of squad cars as they moved in to set up a roadblock on Tuttle Causeway, not far from the mid-island location of his hotel. He assumed all the other causeways were blocked too while the police screened everyone who attempted to leave Miami

Beach in an effort to find the killer of such a prominent citizen as Shelby Bloom.

Affecting nonchalance, Raven strolled into the hotel restaurant and ordered a dinner of broiled pompano and a glass of Chablis. Picking up a discarded *Miami Herald*, he pretended to read it as his mind raced through the possible scenarios involved in escaping. He had no illusions about the intensity of the police search that was certain to follow.

Leaving the restaurant a half hour later, he glanced down the corridor toward Bloom's offices. Various employees scurried about, anxiety and rage apparent on their faces. He wondered if the strike on Bloom would have the desired effect, spreading the flames of the Cerrillo-Gambucci war throughout the drug trafficking and money laundering centered in south Florida, with its tentacles that spread throughout the country.

At that very moment, Marty Gottlieb, nephew and heir apparent to Shelby Bloom, cousin of Nate Gottlieb, and president of the Francone-held bank in California, was immersed in deep discussion with Mario Sanchez, formerly of Colombia, now of Miami Beach.

"Goddamn it, Mario, it looks like we should have listened to Dom Cerrillo when he asked us to hit the Gambucci operations here in Miami. He told us it was only a matter of time before the Gambuccis made a hit on us. Now look, they got Uncle Shelby!"

"Yeah, I know. We should have listened to that mad dog," replied Sanchez, his stilted English heavily accented with his

Colombian Spanish. "But do we really need more violence here? We already have the Cubans forever knocking each other off. We really didn't need a gang war with the Gambuccis. I still think we were right."

"Not now!" yelled Marty. "Not anymore! If we don't hit back now, harder than they ever dreamed, everything we have will be up for grabs. How much muscle can you put out on the streets right away?"

"Enough to blow the Gambuccis off the face of south Florida if you give the word. But just remember—up to now, you and your family have been solid citizens compared to the rest of them. In the eyes of the police, this will put you down at the level of the Gambuccis, not to mention the Rios and the Gonzaleses. There's bound to be hell to pay. I say, go slow."

"No, Mario, with all due respect, you don't understand the psychology of the Gambuccis and the rest. They're a goddamn pack of wolves. As soon as they smell weakness, they turn on the weak ones and tear them up. We've got to strike—immediately!" he shouted, his emotion driving him. He pounded on the table. "Get all your men on the street right now! Hit the Gambuccis and all their Florida affiliates with everything you have. I know if Shelby were alive, that's what he'd order, and that's what I'm ordering, goddamn it!"

"OK, boss. OK. I'll get right on it," replied Sanchez. Secretly, he was already mentally planning to get himself and his family back to Colombia before the war really began.

Back in his room, Raven turned on the television to the cable news channel. The news reports confirmed his fears.

The police had set up roadblocks on all the causeways out of Miami Beach, and they were screening every car. Worse yet, one of the news teams was shown interviewing an elderly woman who described seeing a tall, dark-haired man riding a bicycle and wearing tennis clothes. He had to assume the workers at the bicycle shop would be interviewed and another description added to the first. He was relieved he hadn't used the same name for the bicycle rental as he had checking into the hotel. For now, he decided it was best to simply hole up in the hotel until the normal tourist pressure would cause some loosening of the security around Miami Beach.

He decided that his opportunities for hiding the Ruger would become increasingly worse, so he seized the moment to head down the elevator, out of the hotel, and into the parking lot. Once there, he glanced about to ensure he wasn't being observed. He opened the trunk and then the garment bag and quickly thrust the Ruger inside it. Zipping up the bag, he doubled it over, took it out of the trunk, and strolled back toward the hotel.

Two policemen were interviewing the attendant at the hotel's bicycle rental shop. Raven held his breath, fearing he might be stopped. He walked by them, up the steps and into the lobby, sensing their gazes on his back as he walked away. In the lobby, several more police officers were engaged in a heated discussion with the guard at the doors of Bloom's offices. Apparently, Marty Gottlieb and Mario Sanchez had other business to attend before they were willing to interview the police. Raven crossed the lobby to the elevator.

Back in his room, he breathed a sigh of relief. He quickly

disassembled the Ruger and set its parts in their places in the garment bag, camera bag, and briefcase. Walking out on his balcony, he surveyed the scene spread out before him. Both to the south and to the north he saw pairs of policemen working along the beach, interviewing sunbathers and looking carefully at everyone on the beach. Raven wondered if they'd become so intrusive as to begin room-to-room searches of the hotels along Collins Avenue. *You're being a little paranoid,* he told himself. He took comfort in the fact that the garment bag and briefcase had always passed airport inspections without comment. He decided his primary risk was a positive identification by one of the eyewitnesses he'd bicycled past just after hitting Bloom. He speculated that the police would probably have a composite drawing formulated soon, if they didn't already have one.

He decided to dress as differently as possible from how he'd appeared in his tennis clothes. Removing his jogging suit, he switched into a sport coat and slacks. The urge to walk out of the room, get into the car, and attempt an escape from Miami Beach kept rising. Willing himself to remain out of sight, Raven removed the sport coat, tossed it on the bed, took off his shoes, and turned on the TV.

Unable to concentrate on the TV, he tried to stay calm by thinking of Angela. His thoughts returned to her description of her father and what had happened to him. He finally gave up his attempt at idyllic daydreaming. Deciding to use the time for purposes of continuing his war on the Mafia, he began considering options for future strikes, establishing targets, and making travel plans.

22

FLASH MARUSKA WAS EXCITED. "Henry, look at this!" he exclaimed, shoving a teletype message across Grogan's desk. Grogan read the contents of the message.

"Goddamn, Flash, you just might have been right. Two more hits with a .22 at long range. But what makes you think it isn't some contract hitter hired by the Gambuccis?"

"It's mainly just a feeling I've got. Have you ever seen the Mob operate through solo operators with no apparent backup? I mean, most of the Mob killings I'm aware of have been at close range with pistols, knives, and garrotes and usually with more than one hit man. I'm beginning to think, more and more, that what we have out there is a vigilante. Will you follow up and see if the Miami PD comes up with any brass from the scene? I've got an idea."

"What's that?"

"Well, hopefully make further use of your friend Joyce in statistics with the government strike force. What I'd like to do, if it's a Ruger again, is check Ruger sales around the country against Joyce's list of the Cerrillo victims. If they find any brass, can you see if it matches the Vito Cerrillo brass?"

"Sure thing. I'll get right on it." Reaching for the telephone, Grogan dialed Joyce and learned that she was still working on the victims list and that she should be able to provide it within the next two or three days. As Flash left his office, Grogan was dialing Miami Homicide.

23

NORMALLY CHAOTIC, MATTERS IN THE drug underworld of south Florida erupted into near holo-
caust proportions. Frustrated by his enforced
solitude, Raven took grim pleasure watching TV reports of
various killings by automatic weapons, bombs, and sawed-off
shotguns throughout the area. TV news anchors pointed out
the need for greater law enforcement as the resources of available officers stretched ever thinner.

Back in New York, Flash Maruska began making telephone calls to friends in the armaments business, hoping to
learn the right way to approach Ruger and obtain whatever
warranty lists or other lists of purchasers they might have.
Because of National Rifle Association efforts in Congress,
attempts to attain lists of gun purchasers or warranty cards
from manufacturers would prove difficult, if not impossible,
without the aid of a subpoena. That, in turn, would necessi-
tate some type of law-enforcement action. The problem was
that there was a total absence of leads on a suspect.

Flash considered how Ruger might be approached, con-
templating the pros and cons of the privacy of gun ownership

in America. His ruminations weren't assisted by his stomach. Once again, it was diet time in the Maruska household. The pangs of constriction in a stomach as commodious as that of Flash Maruska were greater than those of a normal human being. Something akin to the toothache of a lion. Flash knew he would be in a testy mood tomorrow. He hoped Henry's inquiries would bring good news in the morning.

After another day of enforced immobility in his room, Raven ventured down to the hotel lobby. His nerves were on edge at the prospect of being surveyed by unidentifiable plainclothes police. Trying to remain calm and inconspicuous, he strolled out of the lobby onto Collins Avenue. He noticed that a southeast wind had picked up. *At least the roar of the surf might help me sleep*, he thought. Looking up and down the avenue, he saw nothing to give him either hope or concern about escaping Miami Beach. He strolled around the block, back to the lobby, and headed back to his room.

There, he switched the TV from channel to channel, attempting to follow the news of erupting gang wars in Florida and up the East Coast. He also listened for reports on the roadblocks and police activity around Miami Beach. Because of the various gangland killings, news of roadblocks or police activity on Miami Beach had waned. Finally, out of frustration, he stripped down to his shorts and began violently exercising in an attempt to tire himself enough to sleep.

24

HENRY GROGAN SAT CRINGING BEHIND HIS battered desk at strike force headquarters. Waves of nausea swept over him. He only knew that for the first time in his life, he dreaded the arrival of his longtime mentor, eating and drinking companion, and partner, Flash Maruska. Various members of the strike force feigned disinterest, studying Henry from the corners of their eyes. Over at the water cooler, he detected a murmur of feminine voices and some surreptitious looks aimed in his direction. Like a condemned prisoner awaiting the guillotine, Henry directed his thoughts to more pleasant subjects: memories of many cases solved and good times with his friend (and secret idol) Flash Maruska.

It did no good. Finally, he sensed the dreaded arrival. At least the agony of waiting was over. The first sound he heard, Maruska's loud voice, talking to the office in general, afforded no solace. "What the hell are you staring at? Let's get to work!"

Henry kept his eyes glued to the paper before him. After an eternity, a huge shadow fell over his desk. Then he heard the creak of his extra chair adjusting to Flash's huge weight. Like a shroud, a silence fell over the room. Henry kept his eyes down as long as he could and then chanced a glance past the corner of the desk. He saw Flash's huge hands twisting a copy of the newspaper into a small rope, the knuckles white. Henry quickly shifted his gaze back to the paper in the center of his desk. Finally, Flash spoke through clenched teeth, his voice uncharacteristically high and tight. His monumental effort at self-control was painfully obvious.

"Henry, how many times have I told you that scumbag Eddie Mulcahey is *not* your friend?" Flash half whispered.

If only he'd yell and pound the desk, thought Grogan.

After a moment, Flash spoke again, in the same tone of voice. "Three hundred times, Henry? Four hundred? Think you could favor me with an answer?"

The combination of his splitting hangover and the controlled rage of his friend began to take its toll on Grogan. He made a stabbing grab for his coffee cup, but his fingers slipped off the handle. He watched with a combination of revulsion and horror as the cup toppled to the floor, shattered with a crash, and splattered coffee over Flash's shoes, socks, and suit pants. "Oh, shit!" mumbled Grogan. He lurched from his swivel chair to his knees as he attempted to wipe up Flash's pants and shoes.

"Stop your fucking self-pity! Goddamn it, I'm trying to have a talk with ya!" Flash yelled.

Henry gave a couple of little kicks at the shards of coffee cup on the floor, went back around his desk, and fell into his chair. One of the greater bonds of the two was a shared sense of humor. Grogan looked again at the newspaper and then back up at Maruska, his red eyes filled with tears of remorse and stifled laughter. Meeting them, Maruska tried biting his tongue, failed to control himself, and finally began shaking with laughter as well.

"Goddamn it, Henry, this time I oughta stay mad. I can't believe you let that fucking Mulcahey loosen your tongue again. You know I love ya, but if you can't get control over your tongue while drinking—I don't know what I'm going to do with you. I've gotta write your efficiency reports. What the hell do you think I can do with a thing like this?" he said, slapping the newspaper in front of Grogan.

The kindness of Flash's tone made Grogan feel worse. Two huge tears welled up in his eyes and rolled down his cheeks. "I don't know what to say. You're right. Maybe I'm a goddamn lush. I dunno. Mulcahey seemed like good company last night. I only thought I'd have a couple of drinks and then go home. I guess I was lonely. He offered to buy me dinner, and the next thing you know, we're gabbing about the gang wars and the killings in Florida and"—he gestured at the paper— "there you are."

They both looked at the headlines, an inch high on the front page of the cheap tabloid popular with New York commuters—VIGILANTE KILLER STALKS MAFIA? Below it, the story outlined how "an informed, unimpeachable source" in the Crime Commission believed the gang wars currently raging had been prompted by a series of hits by an outside vigilante. The rest of the story ran to rank speculation, although the bases of Flash's speculation were also listed, including the facts that the assassinations in New York and Miami had been the work of a solo marksman and how such solo work was uncharacteristic of typical Mob slayings. The possibility of an outside contract assassin was also mentioned, but only at the bottom of the article.

"Do you think we could give a vigilante, if that's what we're dealing with, any better warning?" asked Flash, regaining his composure.

Grogan shook his head sadly. "I'd give you my word that it'll never happen again, but I did that last time. I don't know what to say. Do you want my resignation?"

"I don't know, Henry. I know I don't want it now. I know the last thing I'd ever want is to split us up and see you retire. Police work's your life. But I don't know if I can protect you or even if I should protect you on this one. There's gonna be hell to pay."

"I know. Is there anything I can do? *Anything?*"

"For God's sake, don't get any ideas about trying to undo what you've already said. If you want to do me a favor, get your goddamn work done and get me the list of Cerrillo victims. And if you can figure out some way to get Ruger to give me whatever they have in the way of lists of purchasers, I'd appreciate it," he said gruffly, trying to cover his disappointment—and to suppress the possibility of lapsing again into laughter as he glanced at his stained trousers and the broken pieces of coffee cup on the floor. Finally, he walked around the desk, put his hand on Grogan's shoulder, and said, "First things first, Henry."

"What do you mean?"

"Get your ass down to Walgreens and get an Alka-Seltzer. That's an order."

Grogan got out of his chair, gave Flash a lopsided little smile, and shuffled out. Throughout the office, fellow workers buried their eyes in their work, smiling.

Flash walked out of Grogan's office, his eyes hard. "All right, you bastards," he said to the room, "get your asses back to work. Big things are happening, and we're falling behind." After a moment, typewriters began to clatter and the office sprang to life again.

Back at his desk, Flash contemplated his miserable lunch—an alfalfa sprout and turkey loaf sandwich on pita bread and an orange. Tossing the lunch into the wastebasket, he glanced around surreptitiously and then ambled downstairs to the vending machines to purchase two packages of Hostess Twinkies and a Coca-Cola. Glancing over his shoulder, he wolfed down the Twinkies and washed them down with the soda. Feeling better, he ascended the stairs and returned to his desk, where he pondered the wisdom of a direct call to the head of Ruger.

By that afternoon, all the major wire services had picked up the story from the New York tabloids. Various racketeers and mobsters around the country read the articles and wondered. Sentiment among those already engaged in the conflict was that it made no difference whether the news was true or not. The die had been cast, and the war was on.

Elsewhere, other eyes read the articles, watched the news reports on TV, and heard the speculation on the radio. In

Los Angeles, Carl Johnson saw a newscast about the prospect of a crack marksman vigilante and wondered. Considering the death of Tito Francone, he thought further about the demands of Nate Gottlieb. Finally, he went down to the gun locker in the basement of his home and took out his deer rifle. Working with his crippled right hand and his good left hand, he fumbled with a box of cartridges, attempting to load the rifle with his right hand. He almost gave up. Finally, after dropping many cartridges, he managed to load the rifle. Although the fingers on his right hand were nearly useless for inserting the cartridges, he was able to hold the rifle steady with his good left hand and get his crippled right fingers up to the trigger. After unloading the rifle, he practiced several dry shots at the blocks of the basement wall. Holding the rifle across his knees, he stared at his crippled fingers, thinking.

25

STILL TRAPPED IN HIS HOTEL ROOM ON Miami Beach, Raven heard the first TV reports about the possibility of a vigilante. He wondered what sort of investigation was going on at the organized crime strike force. But he had more immediate concerns. At midmorning, he descended again to the lobby to purchase a newspaper and go to the coffee shop. There he read the latest accounts of gang wars and the roadblocks that had been set up around Miami Beach. He noticed that due to increased tourist pressure, the roadblocks had been modified into a check of suspicious vehicles and persons leaving the area.

The Miami newspapers speculated on the possibilities of a vigilante versus a contract killer. Raven felt some satisfaction that there were at least two theories, rather than certainty that there was an independent vigilante on the loose, waging war on the Mafia.

After finishing his coffee, he walked through the lobby and out onto Collins Avenue. As he surveyed the scene, a car stopped in front of him. Two deeply tanned young men and a woman, all in their early twenties, emerged. They were dressed in sneakers and bathing suits. A surfboard protruded from the right-rear window, which the young people removed. Standing on the corner, they immediately began trying to thumb a ride north. Raven was inspired to action. Turning back to the hotel, he strode rapidly up the steps and across the lobby to the elevator. Back in his room, he hurriedly shed his street clothes, donning his swimsuit, beach shirt, dark glasses, beach cap, and sandals. Shoving his clothes into his luggage, he descended to the lobby and headed out to the parking lot, where he opened the trunk of the car to throw his luggage inside. Minutes later, he left the parking lot and crossed Collins Avenue to the next block. Turning south, he eased down the street two blocks, took a left to Collins Avenue, and turned left again, heading back toward the hotel. Slowing, he had a sinking sensation when he reached the corner where the young hitchhikers had been. They were nowhere to be seen. Cruising slowly north, he felt a surge of relief as he saw them on the next corner, chatting amiably. As he approached, the largest of the boys stuck out his thumb. Raven pulled to the curb. "Heading north?"

"Yeah, we thought with the wind there'd be some surf at South Beach. No such luck," said the smaller of the two boys. "I wish my folks would've stayed in California. The ocean out here sucks."

Raven got out of the car. "What'll we do with that thing?" he asked, gesturing at the surfboard.

"No sweat. We've got ropes and bungees."

Within minutes, they'd tied the surfboard to the top of the vehicle, leaving all four doors open. As they were about to get into the car, Raven casually asked, "Any of you guys got a driver's license? I'm so hungover I'm not sure I can keep the car on the road."

"No sweat, man. I'll handle this rig." The smaller of the boys grinned. The girl giggled.

Raven asked, "How far north do you want to go?"

"Hollywood, man. Ironic, ain't it?"

"I guess so, seeing you're a California guy."

Within minutes, they were moving north on Collins Avenue. Raven slumped in the back, his beach cap pulled over his eyes. As they reached the end of Miami Beach, they approached an intersection. Under the brim of his cap, Raven spotted two policemen standing beside a squad car, checking cars as they passed. After a brief wait, the moment of confrontation arrived. Raven slumped in the back, with his beach cap pulled nearly over his eyes.

"Where you headed?" asked the officer.

"North, back to Hollywood," said the young driver. "Aren't we?" he asked, glancing back at Raven.

Attempting to sound miserably hungover, Raven muttered, "North to Hollywood, yeah."

"North to Hollywood," echoed the older of the two boys.

Carefully checking out the tanned legs of the young lady in front, the trooper gave the order. "OK, move out!"

As they pulled away, Raven slowly exhaled and then settled back as the car moved up the crowded avenue and onto State Road A1A. They drove north past North Miami, North Miami Beach, and on to Hollywood. At Hollywood, he dropped off his passengers, wishing them better surfing in the future. Stopping at a service station, he changed back into street clothes and headed westward to Interstate 95 and then north to Fort Lauderdale–Hollywood International Airport. There, he checked in the car at the rental counter of the National Car Rental, paying cash.

Within an hour, with a one-way ticket to Minneapolis in the name of Charles Hazlet, he boarded a Northwest flight to Minneapolis. By day's end, he was back in Grand Forks, where he retrieved his Ramcharger and returned to the farm. As he drove, he speculated on what he'd accomplished and wondered how long his luck would hold. Trying to put himself in the shoes of the organized crime strike force, he considered what sort of investigations were under way. From his research on the Mafia, he knew the research and investigative resources of the strike force and the FBI were vast.

Always a stickler for detail, Raven knew he'd left spent cartridges from the Ruger at two scenes. He wondered if they'd been found and matched up. He racked his brain over whether or not he'd sent in the warranty card for the Ruger. He was fairly certain he hadn't since he had an excellent memory and he usually recalled sending in such cards. He decided to search for the card when he returned to the farm. Turning fatalistic, he supposed there was little he could do if he'd sent the card in, anyway.

Finally, just as dusk was turning to full dark, he pulled into the farm. As usual, the horses raced him along the fence. Heading out to the corral, he spoke gently as he gave them their oats. "Well, friends, I've done about as much as I can right now for Kari. Now, it's time to look after this place for a while."

Slapping the horses affectionately as he turned them back out to pasture, he walked slowly to the house, taking a deep breath of the sharp, clean northern Minnesota air. It was a contrast to the muggy heaviness of south Florida. Only one name came to mind as he stepped up to the stoop and turned to survey the farm: Dom Cerrillo. "Getting Dom would go a long way toward evening the score," he muttered to himself.

Entering the empty house, he moved into the kitchen, opened the cabinet above the refrigerator, and pulled out a bottle of brandy. He poured himself a healthy glass. Sitting in his rocking chair in the darkened living room, he gazed out across the moonlit farmyard and sipped his brandy. His mind raced from New York, to New Jersey, to Los Angeles, to Miami, and back to New York. *What next?* he mused. Standing, he drained the last of the brandy and headed for bed.

Finally lying in his own bed again, he let the fatigue wash over him. As he drifted off to sleep, his libido took hold of his thoughts, and he relaxed, dreaming of Angela.

26

THE NEXT DAY, HENRY GROGAN SHUFFLED into Flash Maruska's office with a sheaf of computer paper two inches high. "You asked for the most comprehensive list the governor's task force could give us on Cerrillo crime victims. I'm afraid we bit off more than we can chew. This list only goes back three years, and it contains over thirteen hundred names and addresses. Joyce tells me she'll keep cranking, but it's likely to be at least five times this long when complete. Seems the Cerrillos have lots of victims. You want me to continue?"

"Yep. It's all we have to go on for now. If you can keep your goddamn mouth shut, I'll let you in on something. Ruger claims the names of their gun buyers are private, but I think they're willing to check our list against their list and let us know if there are any matches, without fingering anybody specifically. And I'll bet if we get a positive matchup on a likely suspect, they'll confidentially identify *one person* for us. Do you understand the need for absolute secrecy on this?"

"Honest to God, Flash. I've even sworn off the sauce. You've gotta believe me."

"Not even a shot of Bushmills and a beer on Saint Paddy's Day?"

Grogan smiled ruefully. "Well, maybe that."

"I'll tell you what. I can accept a shot of Bushmills and a beer on Saint Paddy's Day, but only on one condition. We have it together." Flash punched Henry gently on the shoulder. "I'd hate to lose a good man, Henry. Not that I give a shit about you personally."

Henry gulped hard and then turned and grabbed the sheaf of paper and shoved it at his friend. "Leave me alone, you big ape. I've got my own snakes and demons to contend with," he said, turning to walk back to his own office.

Flash smiled and buzzed for his secretary. "Break these victims down by crime, by family member involved, and by the branches of the Cerrillos, please," he asked. "I'd like to make some cross references to my charts."

27

THREE DAYS LATER, THE EVENT Flash Maruska had been dreading occurred. Alphonse Angoste, mafioso, porcine gambler, horse-race fixer, and nightclub owner, drove happily along a shell road on the outskirts of New Orleans. He was heading toward his nightclub on the west end of town near the main highway to Baton Rouge. As he pulled into the parking lot, he paid little attention to the pickup truck cruising behind him. After parking, he stepped around his car and headed for the front door as both doors of the pickup opened. After just a glance at the two figures in straw cowboy hats advancing on him, Angoste tried to run. As he did, the first blast of one of the shotguns caught him in the legs, spinning him around and downward onto the white-shell lot of the nightclub. Then the two figures stood over him and blasted nine more rounds from their shotguns into all parts of his body. Moments later, the pickup's tires sprayed shells in all directions as it peeled out of the parking area.

"Dat fix him fo' Papa fo' sho'. Maybe Papa lose the business, but Alphonse don't enjoy it no mo'," spoke a dark, grim-faced man in a heavy Cajun accent.

"Maybe we shoulda left a card—*Courtesy of the Vigilante*," said the other.

The two brothers drove on in silence, deeper and deeper into the Bayou country.

That evening, New Orleans played the story as though the Mafia vigilante had reached New Orleans. Far north of the headwaters of the Mississippi River, Raven sat watching the evening news. Although the possibility of copycat killings had occurred to him, this unexpected dividend took him by surprise. He wondered what effect the New Orleans shooting would have on the deliberations of the FBI, the organized crime strike force, and other investigatory agencies. As he considered this appealing new development, he grimly smiled.

Three days later, another assassination took place in a barroom in Cicero, Illinois. This one featured a rifled shotgun slug fired by a hooded gunman into the abdomen of a vicious loan shark. The shooter then sped away in a stolen taxi. That evening, the national news played the story with the lead "Nation Turns against the Mafia."

Raven followed the news reports with interest, particularly the interview of the Justice Department officials and FBI regional heads throughout the country. *Keep it rolling, folks*, he thought. *Maybe the predators will begin to believe crime really doesn't pay.*

The next day, he headed over to Lorne's house to help service some planting equipment. As they worked with grease guns, Lorne suddenly paused and looked at his brother. "Got a call from New York City today."

"Oh . . . who from?"

"That Lieutenant Massey. The one you got so mad at. Remember him?"

"How can I forget? What did he want?"

"Not much. He said it was just routine. He wanted to know if I or anybody in our family owns a Ruger .22. I told him I don't have one. That's all I told him. You don't either, do you?" Lorne looked quickly at Raven, his blue eyes suddenly bright and animated.

Raven concentrated on his grease gun. "You know, Lorne, it always seems like I miss a few of the zerks when I grease these things."

Lorne walked over, pointing out the zerks Raven had missed. "I never could keep track of all the guns you own. That was always your special thing with Papa, wasn't it?"

"Yeah. I really liked working on those guns with him."

An hour later, they'd finished greasing the equipment and were washing up in the corner of Lorne's spotless pole barn. As he wiped his hands, Raven gazed out the door across Lorne's yard to the beautiful fields beyond. "Looks like it might be a good year," he said. "Just the right amount of moisture in the soil, I think." As he walked away, Raven looked directly at his brother. "I think maybe one time I had a Ruger .22, some time ago. But I'm sure I don't own one anymore."

"I didn't think so. Anyway, the lieutenant didn't specify what he meant by family. I think he must have meant just my immediate family."

"You never can tell about those New York people."

"Nope. You sure can't figure them," said Lorne, watching his brother stroll out of the shop, across the yard, and through the woods to his home. As he melted into the woods, Lorne remembered how much Kari had loved Raven. Fighting back tears, he bit his lip and headed into the house.

28

B Y THE END OF THE WEEK, THINGS WERE really getting out of hand around the country. In the Chicago area alone, several minor mafiosi had seized the opportunity created by the confusion to make hits on rival families who, in their opinions, had poached on their turf. Retaliatory strikes were then made, and a minor war began to flare up among three Chicago families. Then on Saturday there were two long-range rifle slayings of Mafia figures in Buffalo, New York, and Tucson, Arizona.

Back in his office, Maruska sat with Henry Grogan. "At least we know that one and maybe both of these rifle shootings in Buffalo and Tucson weren't by my vigilante," offered Flash. "That is, unless he owns his own private Learjet!"

"Goddamn. I'm sorry, Flash. I had no idea my big mouth would result in something like this."

"Well, I'm feeling kinda philosophical about it. Don't take that the wrong way, though. I mean, we both know what our duty is and what we're sworn to do. We both know as good cops we can never tolerate vigilantism in any form. We know it can lead to chaos. On the other hand, I guess I don't get quite as worked up about these killings as I might about an ax murder at a Sunday-school picnic. From my records, not a single mafioso who has been killed thus far has less than three killings attributable to him. And some—Shelby Bloom, for instance—go back to Prohibition and have the blood of scores of victims on their hands."

Pondering the situation, Henry nodded. "Yeah, I guess I can't feel too bad if some of these assholes we'd like to send to the chair get blown away. Particularly those who've been thumbing their noses at us for years. But that won't stop us from trying to bring in this vigilante, will it, Flash?"

"You know me better than that. But maybe after I put the cuffs on him, I might shake his hand."

"I hope I'm there to see it. I mean, we aren't exactly staggering under the weight of prosecuting all our collars."

"I know. I've got some hunches that I want to play. Mind the fort. I'm heading over to NYPD Homicide. If you need me, I'll be talking to Massey."

29

NGELA SIMONE BEGAN RUNNING FOR THE telephone as soon as it rang and then caught herself and let it ring three times before she picked up. Nevertheless, she was slightly breathless as she answered. *God, I hate myself when I act like this*, she thought. *It's probably just another student.* When she heard Raven's voice, her pulse quickened, and she flushed. "Next weekend at your place?" she echoed. "Well, I've got a lot of papers to correct—oh, shit, I'm not going to be coy with you. Of course, I'd love it! Can we go horseback riding again?"

"Yep, the horses miss you. And so do I. If you're really good, I might even bake you a blueberry pie."

"I thought I *was* really good." Angela laughed.

"You're the best. I can almost guarantee you a piece of pie."

"I promise to be on my *best behavior*. How should we handle the driving?"

"I'll drive in to get you early Saturday morning. When do you have to be back?"

"Well, I don't have any classes until afternoon Monday. Do you think you can put up with me both Saturday and Sunday nights?"

"I'm willing to make the sacrifice," answered Raven.

Both were delighted at how easily their conversation went after not seeing one another for several weeks.

The next Saturday, they had an idyllic day, riding the horses around the farm and then across some wooded and marshy state land that stretched north from the Ravendal farm all the way to the Canadian border. At noon, Raven led them to a clearing on a knoll deep in some ancient spruces, surrounded by alder and cedar swamp. To reach this spruce "island," the horses had been forced to wade on an old corduroy road for the last quarter mile.

"It's beautiful in here!" Angela exclaimed. "Did someone used to live here?"

"No. But long ago, my father, Lars, and some of his friends logged out here one winter. This clearing was the campsite. They logged down in the cedars and in that spruce swamp over there. My dad told me that with that logging money he raised his initial stake to make a down payment on most of our land, other than the original homestead. I don't think anybody really remembers or comes here anymore other than me. Look over there," he said, pointing.

Angela turned to see a family of ruffed grouse walking under a huge spruce at the edge of the clearing. "They seem as tame as chickens," she said.

"They've never seen a human before. Like I say, I don't think anyone knows about the place, except me and maybe a couple old-timers that used to work with Dad, if they're still alive. Ruffed grouse are tricky fliers when they're startled. But if they don't see people, they become very tame."

Angela looked at him. "Hold me, Raven," she said suddenly.

Instantly, they were together, mouths open, tasting each other again. As one, they sank to the ground. Then, naked beneath the northern sky, they made love again, open to one another as never before. The wildness of the surroundings heightened all their senses as their bodies entangled, each trying to get ever closer. The passion of the time and place and their eager bodies rose like a river in flood, as they thrust again and again at one another, completely enraptured.

Finally spent, they lay on their sides, gazing into one another's eyes. Neither spoke as their shining eyes locked and they rested side by side, arms gently touching, not wanting to break the spell of the place and the moment. Then, they both began to smile, pulling together again, gently rocking. Very gently, they repeated their loving, this time infinitely tender. Then both drifted into a deep sleep. Later, awakening together, they stood up, helped each other dress, mounted the horses, and silently rode away, neither willing to speak. That evening, back at the house, Angela leaned back in Raven's arms as they watched the flames leap in his fireplace.

"Tell me again about your father," Raven invited.

Angela retold the entire story—how close she and her father had been, how she was the most faithful member of the family in her visits to him in prison, and how devastated she was when he was murdered.

After she finished, Raven asked, "How certain are you that Dom Cerrillo ordered the murder?"

"As certain as I can possibly be, based on my family connections and everything I learned about the story while I was a prosecutor—and later, when I studied the Mafia in the course of my work at the law school."

"Do you think there's any possibility he'll ever pay?"

"Not on this earth. Not enough. I mean, I believe the RICO Act is a great tool to hurt the Mafia financially, but it seems as if the ones giving the orders for the hits never get prosecuted for murder. Sometimes they serve time for tax evasion or extortion or labor racketeering or something like that. But despite their violence, they rarely seem to pay for their acts of violence as such. And with a situation like a Mob hit on another Mob member, the chances of prosecution are very slim. It used to keep me awake nights, thinking about my dad. And whenever the subject comes up, it enrages me all over again. But I guess I've reconciled myself to the idea that justice will never be done in the case of Carlo Simone. Why do you ask?" she inquired, her eyebrows raised.

"Because of how I felt when I learned about my niece, Kari. She was like a daughter to me. So I wondered how you feel about the man behind your loss."

For a long time, they both stared into the flames, lost in their thoughts.

After a few minutes, Raven ventured, "Did you ever think about personally taking revenge on Dom Cerrillo or the men who actually made a hit on your dad?"

"I used to dream about it, again and again. In fact, I still fantasize about getting even with that sneering, evil man!" The intensity of Angela's outburst surprised both of them. "I'm sorry, Raven; the question brings out something primitive in me. To be perfectly honest, if I had the chance right now, I really believe in my heart of hearts that I could kill him without a twinge," she added.

"I know how you feel," he said.

As silence fell over them again, the flames in the fireplace crackled higher. Raven's hand grasped her clenched fist, and he squeezed tightly as they continued to watch the fire, each caught up in a particular vision.

Later, Raven shared, "You know, Angela, I've given the matter quite a bit of thought. It seems to me, throughout the centuries, whenever powerful, evil men have been willing to use violence to achieve their ends—and good men shy away from returning violence with violence—the evil ones prevail.

"I remember a saying from my old history books about the Viking raiders demanding danegeld, a ransom, to stay away. The saying goes that paying danegeld only gets rid of one thing: the geld. But it never gets rid of the Dane. Big cities have grown so tolerant of vice and corruption and everything that goes with it that they tolerate the barbarians in their midst. At least in part because they aren't willing to pay the price to purge the barbarian. As I understand it, that was often the case on the frontier, too. Nowadays, it seems true wherever there's a big market for illegal activity, such as gambling or drugs. In these situations, it seems as if the law is completely ineffectual when it comes to catching and punishing the evilest predators. Out here, where the population is sparse and we live more in the open, we have our own way of dealing with them."

"You never lived in the city, Raven. You have no experience of how insidious organized crime can be. You're right about society looking the other way at many of the illegal activities that finance the criminals. Where I grew up, gambling on the numbers, gambling on athletics, off-hours drinking, untaxed cigarettes, fixed political jobs, drugs, and prostitution were part of everyday life. And it's true that since they were illegal, the toughest crooks eventually prevailed. From my studies, I'm certain that's how the Mob got started in America, during Prohibition. But the bottom line for me was that the only hope at making any dent at all in the Mafia was to become a prosecutor. And eventually, after struggling against the indifference and corruption of New York, I guess I finally withdrew to my academic ivory tower. At least when I teach my students about the RICO Act, I'm enlarging the circle of people willing to take a financial shot at the Mob."

As they lay in bed that night, Raven ventured, "Angela, if I was ever charged with committing a crime involving taking revenge, would you defend me?"

"Um, why are you asking?"

"I don't know . . . it just seems sort of symmetrical, given our relative experiences."

"I've been educated to champion the idea—and I've always believed—that everyone deserves a defense under the law. If you think I could give you the best defense, of course I'd defend you."

Raven smiled. "You'd be amazed if you knew how good that makes me feel. Let's hope it never comes to pass. But if it does, I know I'd have the most dedicated lawyer in the world on my side."

Late that night, as Raven lay sleeping beside her, Angela gently touched the strange wound on Raven's shoulder as she looked out the window. She watched the tops of the pines at the edge of the woods, swaying in the wind. Putting her arms around Raven's chest, she buried her head tightly in his back as she murmured, "I'd do anything you asked. Anything." Then digging her fingers into his body, she began rhythmically pulling at the muscles of his abdomen and chest. Aroused, he turned to her as she fell savagely upon him. His passion mounting to meet hers, they began to make love again with an elemental intensity neither had ever known. At the end, bathed in the sweat of their ardor, they both spoke the same words, simultaneously. "God, I love you."

The next week, Angela received a telephone call from Grand Forks International Airport. "I'm heading out to New York again on business," said Raven. "I shouldn't be gone over a week. When I get back, I'd like to see you again. OK?"

"I'd love it! What shall we do?"

"This time, you decide. Why don't you check out the concerts and plays in Winnipeg? This time of year, there's quite a bit going on up there."

"You're on," she said.

As she heard the click of the telephone disconnecting, she wondered again about Gunar Ravendal. There had been something strange in his voice—something almost . . . conspiratorial. Shrugging it off, she returned to her work, happy with the prospect of being reunited with him on his return.

30

August 1977

RAVEN REPEATED HIS PATTERN OF TRAVEL, buying a ticket from Grand Forks to Chicago in his own name. In Chicago, he purchased a ticket to Kennedy Airport in the name of Roger Fromelt. There he rented a car, using his California identification. From Kennedy, he drove north on Interstate 678 until he crossed the East River and then headed north again on Interstate 95, paralleling the western shore of Long Island Sound all the way to Connecticut. Near Norwalk, he headed north on Route 7 until he reached the vicinity of the Cerrillo estate. Drawing on knowledge obtained from newspapers and the organized crime strike force publications he'd studied, he drove through the rolling hills of southwestern Connecticut. He passed stone walls, orchards, small lakes, and streams. As he drove away from the coast, the country grew higher and rougher. Reaching the small town nearest the Cerrillo estate, Raven checked into a motel at its outskirts, with the same ID he'd used for the car.

In the hotel room, he began assembling his arsenal and equipment. This time, he assembled the .270 Winchester, complete with scope, as well as the sawed-off shotgun. In addition, he carried a razor-sharp Finnish fish knife in a sheath, a garrote made of steel wire with a wooden handle on each end, five railroad flares, a lighter, and a small, powerful flashlight. After determining his equipment was in good order, he hid it again in his luggage and replaced it in the trunk of his car.

Returning to the room, he donned hiking boots, a tweed hat commonly used by bird watchers, a khaki jacket, and blue jeans. Taking along a pair of binoculars, he drove the car close to the Cerrillo estate. Entering a small woods, he found a hardwood walking stick about four feet in length. He walked farther into the woods, about a quarter mile from the estate house, moving slowly, pausing occasionally to observe various birds through the binoculars. As he observed birds, he would stop and use the walking stick to steady a notebook, upon which he would record the date and species observed. Gradually, he worked himself through the woods to a point about six blocks from the road, but only about ten feet from the fence surrounding the estate.

It was a ten-foot cyclone fence, topped by four strands of barbed wire. Above the top strand of barbed wire, he observed another thin wire, supported by insulators, designed to carry an electrical charge. Looking both directions down the fence, Raven spotted small boxes equipped with electric eyes set on the tops of posts at fifty-foot intervals. The boxes didn't swing from side to side but rather were trained at angles downward along the fence, presumably setting up a field of electronic surveillance and an alarm system along the edge of the fence, all the way around the perimeter of the farm.

Using his binoculars, he swept the perimeter and observed that the fence system surrounded the entire farm. Along the road, the harshness of the cyclone fence was mitigated somewhat by a white, wooden rail fence, set approximately five feet outside it, running to a guardhouse at the main gate. A driveway wound approximately two hundred yards to the garage and the imposing, fieldstone and white clapboard manor house, flanked by stables and garages situated around a circular courtyard.

Through the lens of his binoculars, Raven was startled to see two dark shapes streaking toward him. The speed with which the two black-and-tan Dobermans covered the ground from the farmhouse to the fence amazed him. The dogs stopped about five feet from the fence, where they stood, snarling. Not wishing to be noticed by the guard, Raven slowly turned and sauntered deeper into the woods, ignoring the dogs. After snarling at him for a few seconds, the dogs trotted along the fence toward the road, paralleled the road to the guardhouse, and then ran back to the courtyard area of the farmhouse. Raven kept working farther away from the road, toward the rear of the Cerrillo property. As he walked along the fence, he noted that no tree branches crossed it, but many of the trees next to it were considerably higher than the fence. Near the corner of the fence farthest from the road, Raven encountered a small stream that bubbled out of the hills behind the farm and headed at an angle toward the highway. The stream gurgled merrily over a sandy bottom and seemed to have few pools. In most places, it ran over rocks at a depth of less than a foot.

Moving along the back fence, Raven walked toward a small knoll behind the Cerrillo property. Taking care not to skyline himself, he sat on a rock about halfway up the knoll. It was extremely doubtful that he was observed from this location. From the knoll, he could scan nearly the entire property with his binoculars. Taking out the notebook, he carefully diagramed the location of all the buildings. Then, moving the lenses slowly from one side of the property to the other, he began drawing in every possible bit of cover, marking rocks, small depressions in the terrain, bushes, rises, trees, and corners of all the buildings. He took great pains to include all details he could observe from the knoll. Then on a second page, he drew in the windows, doors, gables, woodpiles, vehicles, and equipment visible from his vantage point. Having exhausted everything he could see from the knoll, Raven hiked at an angle away from the farm and then paralleled the back fence to a point near its next far corner. He removed his notebook and, with the aid of the binoculars, completed his mapping and diagraming from the new angle. He could see a long, white machine shed that had been converted into a five-car garage, separated from the main house by about twenty feet. Between the garage and the house, he saw what he'd been looking for: a powerful diesel generator that would provide electricity in the event of a power failure. The generator sat under a small roof designed to protect it from the weather. It appeared to be wired to the house through a steel conduit that ran along the ground for a distance of about fifteen feet.

Raven continued his survey of the perimeter of the property, moving along the fence back down to the highway. Looking up, he noted utility poles running along the roadside nearest the estate. At a point approximately 150 feet from the guardhouse, he saw a lead running down a pole to a junction box, which sat between the white rail fence and the cyclone fence. Electric service to the manor house apparently ran underground, since there were no utility poles running from the junction box to the farmhouse. The cable running down the utility pole and underground to the junction box was sheathed in heavy plastic.

After completing his notes of the terrain from this last vantage point, Raven moved back over the same route he'd initially taken, pausing from time to time at different angles to complete his notation of bushes, rocks, furrows, and other cover. Occasionally, he saw the guard at the main gatehouse leave the house and walk around. When he reached the rear of the farm, Raven headed back, deeper into the woods, scouting the terrain behind the farmhouse. As he moved back, the terrain grew rougher, with higher hills and bushy ravines. Paralleling the brook, he encountered several small brooks and rivulets feeding it from both sides. He mapped the general area as he moved along.

About a mile behind the knoll, he scaled a hill topped by a stand of ancient white pines. Raven climbed the tallest of the white pines until he reached a point where he could survey the woods for several miles around. Taking out the notebook, he mapped the area carefully for about twenty minutes. Descending the tree, he made his way back to the small knoll behind the estate and took a concealed ground position that afforded a good field of observation through the binoculars. His pulse quickened as he scanned the courtyard: Dom Cerrillo's limousine was parked opposite the garage. Apparently, the limousine had either arrived or been removed from the garage when he'd been surveying the country behind the farm. After about fifteen minutes, one of Dom's bodyguards came out of the house, opened the garage door, and parked the limousine. Through the garage door, Raven made out a four-wheel-drive vehicle equipped with a snowplow in the bay next the limousine. From his angle, he couldn't see if more vehicles occupied any of the other stalls.

At four o'clock, there was a change of guards. The replacement guard came out of the house, walked to the garage, and opened the far garage door. He pulled out in an electric golf cart, which he drove down to the main gate. The relieved guard drove the golf cart back to the garage and then walked back into the house. Raven surmised that the guard probably changed every eight hours. Noting that Dom Cerrillo had traveled with two bodyguards when he'd observed him in New York, he concluded that there must be at least two more guards inside the house, in addition to Dom. Raven continued his surveillance for another half hour, hoping to get a better fix on the number of occupants in the house.

At about six o'clock, a stunning blonde figure in Levi's emerged carrying two dog dishes. As if on cue, the Dobermans trotted up and began to devour the dog food. The blonde returned to the house and emerged a few minutes later with a large water dish, which she placed between the dog food dishes. As she bent over, the kitchen door opened, and Raven spotted Dominick Cerrillo watching her. The blonde looked up and, hearing herself being summoned back to the house by Cerrillo, quickly went back inside. Raven wondered whether anyone else had accompanied Cerrillo—other than his bodyguards, the guardhouse men, and the blonde. Waiting about an hour, he saw no more movement.

Traffic on the road running in front of the property was sparse. Occasionally, he noted police cars slowly passing. He wondered if the place was regularly watched by law-enforcement agencies. It appeared that at least during daylight hours, a police car moved along the road about every forty minutes. Closing his notebook, he moved stealthily back to his car.

Rather than driving back past the guard gate, he continued along the road to the next town. There, he found a convenience store and gas station. After filling the tank with gas, he entered the building and walked to the tool section at the rear of the store. He selected a heavy woodman's ax and sharpening stone, which he purchased along with the gas. After completing his purchases, he retraced his route along the road past the Cerrillo estate. Across the road from the guardhouse, a plantation for Norway pines, all about twenty-five feet high, stretched back as far as he could see. About half a mile down the road, farmhouses sat on both sides of the road. From this point, the hobby farms grew somewhat smaller all the way back to the town where his motel was located.

31

AS RAVEN RETURNED TO HIS MOTEL ROOM, a black Ford sedan pulled into the yard of one of the hobby farms between the town and Cerrillo estate. Carrying pizzas and a six-pack of diet cola, FBI Agents White and Bridges entered the farmhouse through the kitchen door and headed into the dining room. There they found Agents Jeter and Carbone sitting in front of a switchboard. Each wore headphones and had logs and report forms spread out before them. A slender, sandy-haired Southerner, White drawled, "Anything new across the wires, boys?"

"Two more long-distance calls, one from New York and one from Miami," replied Jeter, smiling. "It seems the wars rage on." Jeter was a huge black man with enormous forearms and biceps. "I don't know who set 'em off, but they sure as hell know how to kill each other. I wish to hell Cerrillo knew some adjectives other than *motherfuck* and *fuckin*'," he added. "Guess it shows what a wasted youth can do. I wonder if our friend Dom ever reads anything besides balance sheets and comic books."

Agent Bridges, a stocky, dark-haired man with a Boston accent, spoke up. "You guys gonna get some shut-eye between now and midnight?"

Carbone answered, "We'll just have a little pizza and then turn in about eight. I don't know if I can get to sleep this shift. Maybe I'll head into town and do a little shopping. You coming, Jeter?"

"Yeah, I'd like to get out of here before we go back on dogwatch. Let's move."

White donned Carbone's headphones as Bridges logged in the start of their shift. The two teams were alternating six-hour shifts, which they'd been doing for the past week. As their reports were completed, they were sent via a portable facsimile machine that sat on the dining room table to FBI headquarters in both New York and Washington. There, they were available for use by the FBI, the organized crime strike force, and other law-enforcement agencies on a need-to-know basis.

In his motel room, Raven laid out his clothes and equipment. In addition to his hunting boots, he set out a pair of black jeans, black turtleneck sweater, dark-brown leather jacket, black ski mask, black leather gloves, and stocking cap. He coiled the garrote and secured it with a small piece of electrician's tape and then slipped the coiled wires over his head. Satisfied with the size of the loop, he set it alongside the other equipment. Then he attached a sling to the .270 Winchester and practiced looping it across his back, adjusting the sling until it rested snugly against his shoulders. Next, he added a long leather holster, equipped to secure the sawed-off shotgun to his leather belt. He filled two bandoliers with shotgun shells and took out a leather pouch. He set the railroad flares in the bottom of the pouch, along with a butane lighter. Next, he took the stone and honed the Finnish fillet knife. Using the same stone, he gave his new ax a razor-sharp edge. Then he took out his diagrams and made one last, thorough study of the Cerrillo property and surrounding terrain. Satisfied with his preparations, he rose and walked outside to check the weather.

It was a lovely spring evening. A full moon was just rising. As he left the motel and headed down the walk, the Ford, carrying agents Jeter and Carbone, cruised by. Neither Raven nor the two agents had any idea that within hours, their fates would be intertwined.

32

A T FOUR THE NEXT MORNING, Raven awoke and forced himself to eat a breakfast of two granola bars and a pint of milk. He shoved four more granola bars and a canteen of water into the leather pouch, quickly dressed himself in his black clothing, and left the motel. Putting all his weaponry and equipment in the back seat of the car, he drove past the Cerrillo estate to the point where the stream crossed the road.

Near the stream, an old driveway crossed the ditch. Raven pulled into it and drove about fifty feet into the woods, where he left the car. Donning the gloves, ski mask, and cap, he was now completely clothed in black and dark brown from head to foot. Swiftly, he donned the bandoliers and slung the pouch on his right hip, the garrote around his neck, and the .270 across his back. Next, he shoved the shotgun into its holster on his left thigh. This left his hands free to carry the ax.

He locked the car and quietly walked back to the edge of the road. It was a soft spring night, with a gentle, southerly breeze. Moonlight gently illuminated the open areas, although the woods were clothed in deep shadow. In a little over an hour, it would be daylight. Quickly crossing the road,

Raven entered the Norway pine plantation. He walked back into the trees about two hundred feet and then moved parallel to the road across from the front fence of the Cerrillo property. As he reached a point opposite the guardhouse, he noted that it was illuminated by a small spotlight. The yard of the estate house was lit with one large yard light.

Moving beyond the guard gate about fifty yards, he removed the rifle and watched the guard through the scope. The stocky, dark-haired man wore headphones and was gently moving his head in time to music as he read a magazine. Satisfied that the guard wasn't looking in his direction, Raven swiftly crossed the road, ax in hand. With one sharp strike, he severed the electric cable at the base of the utility pole. Instantly, all the lights in the guardhouse and the estate house went out. Leaving the ax, Raven moved swiftly toward the guardhouse, removing the garrote from around his neck as he covered the ground with long, lithe strides. The guard was looking out the window toward the farmhouse as he dialed the number of the electric company. Raven silently entered the guardhouse behind him. The last memory the guard had was the feeling of the wire cutting into his neck. Death came swiftly as he slumped to the floor.

Raven quickly coiled the garrote and shoved it into his pouch. Then he stepped out of the guardhouse and moved at an angle toward a small rise about fifty yards from the main house. Unslinging the .270, he scanned the house with the scope. There appeared to be no movement inside it. Sensing danger, he glanced to his left and stiffened as he saw the black shapes of the two Dobermans hurtling toward him. Startled, Raven managed to pick up the lead dog in his scope and fired. The dog tumbled forward and then lay still. The second dog charged on. As it approached him, Raven knew it was too close for the scope. He snapped off a shot, which missed by inches. Then the dog was airborne, leaping at him. Raven couldn't work the bolt quickly enough to get off another shot. He jabbed the rifle barrel at the dog, deflecting its leap. The dog circled him, snarling. Raven unsheathed his razor-sharp knife. He shoved the rifle out toward the dog and felt instant pain as its powerful jaws closed over his left hand. Striking in a ripping motion with the fillet knife, he plunged the blade deeply into the dog's body, up through the stomach, finally piercing its heart. Slowly the jaws released, and the eviscerated dog fell to the ground.

Quickly returning the knife to its sheath, Raven switched the rifle to his right hand and moved the fingers of his left hand. Although the punctures from the dog's canine teeth stung, the fingers and muscles of his hand were still in working order. Dropping to one knee, he swept the house with the scope. Although he detected no movement, he reasoned that the absence of the usual electric noises and the yard light would soon awaken at least some, maybe all, of its occupants. Using the irregularities of the terrain for maximum cover, he worked his way in a series of short rushes until he reached the edge of the garage. Then, dropping to all fours, he crept to the edge of the generator, about twenty feet from the house. Reaching forward, he tore out all its spark plug wires, throwing them on the ground behind him. He crouched behind the generator, watching the house. Directly before him, beside the conduit from the generator, he saw a second conduit for the main electrical service. Next to that was a black telephone wire. Glancing at the house and detecting no movement, he moved quickly to the edge of the house, removed his knife, and cut the phone wire.

At the hobby farm, agent Carbone removed his headphone. "Jeter, there's something funny going on at the Cerrillo place. About five minutes ago, somebody started dialing something. Then I got a busy signal, like there was a phone off the hook. Now, all of a sudden, the lines have gone dead. I wonder if it's an interruption of service or if something's going down."

"Check with the phone company right away!" replied Jeter.

Crouched beside the house, Raven heard movement and then a shout. "Power's out!" shouted one of Dom's bodyguards.

Instantly, Raven heard Dom Cerrillo snarl, "Start the goddamn generator then. That's what we got it for. Do I have to do everything around here?"

Raven resumed his position behind the generator. Setting the rifle on the ground, he uncoiled the garrote. A burly figure bustled out the kitchen door and up to the generator, carrying a flashlight. He looked at the torn spark plug wires and began exclaiming "What the—" as the steel wire encircled his neck.

After the guard was down, Raven picked up the rifle again, waiting.

At their posts, Carbone and Jeter pondered their situation. "The phone company says the problem must be at the Cerrillo estate. There's no sign of an interruption of service anywhere up and down the line," Jeter reported.

"I wonder if we should call the locals, or get instructions from headquarters, or go to the farm ourselves, or what?" replied Carbone.

"Better call headquarters. I'd hate to blow something important by sending in the locals."

Carbone dialed FBI headquarters in New York, hoping someone with authority was on duty. Simultaneously, the emergency operator at the telephone company, alerted by the call from the FBI agents, was placing a call to emergency repairs in the next town.

Raven continued his vigil by the generator, listening intently for noises from the house. Within seconds, the kitchen door opened, and a second figure emerged. This time, the man was crouched, with a cocked .357 Magnum in his hand. Raven had the advantage of knowing his location, and as the bodyguard raised his pistol, a 180-grain bullet from the .270 caught him full in the chest. He pitched backward, dead before he hit the ground. Almost immediately, the glass in the window opposite the generator shattered as the guard, armed with a submachine gun, broke the pane and began sweeping the area with automatic fire.

The first rays of dawn mingled with the waning moonlight, giving slightly better light for Raven. The battle heightened as Raven fired a blast of his shotgun through the window, covering a dash to the shrubbery in front of the house. Immediately, he heard the remaining guard shout to Dominick, "I located one of 'em! He's got a shotgun! I think I heard a rifle, too! They're out by the garage! Can you see anything from upstairs?"

As he shouted, Raven removed one of the railroad flares and lighter. Lighting the flare, he smashed the front window and threw the flare inside. The living room filled with blinding light. Immediately, he smashed through the window and opened fire, raking the room with buckshot from his shotgun. The first blast caught the guard in the abdomen, and he doubled over, only to be blown backward with a second blast to the head. Raven dove to his left into a study, just before a blast of automatic weapon fire from Dom Cerrillo's submachine gun filled the living room. From somewhere upstairs, he heard a woman screaming.

A telephone utility truck drove up the road and pulled up to the guardhouse. As the driver approached the building, he heard firing up at the main house. Then his gaze fell upon the body of the guard sprawled out on the floor, his hand clutching the telephone. Turning white, he spun around and ran back to the van. With a grinding of gears, he tore away.

The large estate house was silent, except for the muffled sobbing of a woman's voice upstairs. Raven's left hand was beginning to ache and sting from the dog bite.

As Dom Cerrillo retreated to the bedroom, he fired bursts of searching fire down through the floor of the ancient house. Several rounds penetrated the carpeting and flooring, striking dangerously close to Raven. Raven immediately pulled back into the fireplace in the study. As he did so, Cerrillo's young, blonde companion began screaming again. Glancing out the window, Raven saw the sun begin to peek over the line of trees across the road from the guardhouse.

33

ACK AT THEIR POSTS, THE FBI AGENTS had made
contact with their New York headquarters. The duty
officer advised them to alert the Connecticut State
Police and coordinate activities with them. While these calls
were happening, Flash Maruska was just finishing his shower.
As he dressed and prepared to make his way to the office, he
had one of his famous hunches: *Today is going to be a big
day. Something important is going down in the Mob investigation.* Flash walked from the bedroom to the kitchen, trying to beat Rosalee to the refrigerator, where he knew there
was some leftover steak from the night before. His face fell as
he confronted his beaming wife and looked at the breakfast
table. "Surprise, dear!" she exclaimed. "I've made you some
nice grapefruit compote and dry toast to go with your black
coffee. I wouldn't want my honey to have a heart attack!"

"What if your honey fainted from hunger and had a wreck
on the expressway?"

After wolfing down the pitiful breakfast, he got into his
government-issue sedan and headed for the freeway.

34

ROUCHED IN THE FIREPLACE, Raven desperately
considered his situation. Neither his .270 nor the
chopped shotgun were adequate weapons, head to
head, against Dom's submachine gun. He needed to create
a diversion. Glancing around the room, his gaze fell upon a
canister of Georgia fatwood kindling. Bookcases flanked the
fireplace. Just in front of the bookcase, to the right of the fireplace, was a magazine rack. Grabbing a newspaper from the
rack, he crumpled its pages into large balls, throwing them
into the corner. Taking his lighter from his pouch, he lit the
newspapers, throwing fatwood into the flames. Within seconds, flames were licking up the corner of the wall, igniting
the magazines. Soon the books began to burn. Turning the
other direction, he took the rest of the fatwood and some
more newspaper and placed it under the window curtains on
the far wall. He repeated the ignition, and soon the curtains
burst into flames. It was only a matter of seconds before the
flames and smoke began filtering up into the bedroom.

Raven took a deep breath and then hurled himself out of
the study. Back in the main living room, he took a position

behind a heavy leather sofa, beside the body of the dead guard. The study began to fill with flames. Smoke billowed out of its open doorway into the living room.

Suddenly, the blonde woman appeared at the head of the staircase. "Don't shoot! Don't shoot me!" she shouted.

"Get out of here, fast!" Raven shouted at her. As she ran down the steps, Raven detected movement, and he dove for cover behind the kitchen wall. Instantly, a burst of machine-gun fire tore into the couch where he'd been hiding. Lying on his stomach, Raven quickly glanced to the head of the staircase. Seeing nothing, he pulled back into the kitchen and moved silently across it to an alcove below the staircase. As he passed the kitchen window, he spotted the blonde frantically driving out of the driveway in Cerrillo's limousine.

Down on the highway, a joint convoy of state police officers, county sheriff's deputies, and FBI agents was approaching the estate. They moved deliberately, without sirens and flashers, not knowing what they'd encounter other than the dead guard. As they approached the main gate, the limousine careened out of it ahead of them, showering gravel from the shoulder as it took a sharp left turn and headed toward town.

County Sheriff Clayton Winslow, driving the lead vehicle, spotted the limousine and immediately radioed the rest of the caravan that he was giving chase. Turning on his flashers, he pressed down on the accelerator. Then, glancing to his left, up the hill toward the estate house, he saw the flames leaping out of the study window. He radioed the convoy. "It looks like a fire up there at the main house. Someone contact the fire department." The remaining police vehicles converged on the guardhouse.

Raven crouched beneath the staircase, waiting for an opportunity to get Dom Cerrillo. Great clouds of smoke were beginning to fill the house. Suddenly, bursts of machine-gun fire began filling the room as Dom Cerrillo, coughing, came to the head of the staircase. Blinded by the smoke and enraged by the attack on his house, Dom was, characteristically, a raving beast.

"Come on out, ya motherfucker! Son of a bitch, come on out and fight, goddamn ya!" he yelled. As he did so, Raven stepped out and fired a blast from the shotgun. The charge caught the capo in the belly, and he lurched forward, tumbling down the stairs. The machine gun clattered down alongside him. At the bottom of the stairs, he lurched to his knees, clutching his bloody stomach.

"Who the fuck are ya, goddamn ya?" he screamed.

Gunar Ravendal stepped toward Dom as flames and smoke arose around them. "You don't know me, but you attacked my family, and I hit back. You had my niece killed. Her name was Kari Ravendal. And long ago, you had a man named Carlo Simone killed in prison. Now it's your turn to die."

Dom's eyes widened with the mention of Simone. Then, his features contorted with rage, he dove for the machine gun. Again, the blast of Raven's shotgun filled the room. This time, the full charge tore into Dom Cerrillo's chest, and he sprawled back against the bottom steps of the staircase, eyes wide, lips curled back in a snarl that froze on his face in death.

At the foot of the hill, the police officers were conferring. In the background, they could hear the sound of fire sirens. As they debated their plan of action, Raven dashed out the kitchen door, stooping by the generator to grab his .270 as he left. It was almost full daylight. Looking down the hill toward the road, he saw the police cars massed at the foot of the driveway. Quickly, he looked around for an escape route. As he did so, as if on command, the police cars began to move slowly up the driveway, with officers on foot fanning out behind the lead vehicles.

Raven dashed into the garage and ran for the four-wheel-drive Jeep that was equipped with a snowplow. After throwing open the garage door, he leaped inside the vehicle. His heart was pounding with the prospect of being caught. Frantically, he looked for keys. Seeing none in the ignition, he reached beneath the floor mat. Again, nothing. Desperation welling up inside him, he checked the visor. The keys tumbled into his lap. Jamming the keys into the ignition, he started the engine and backed it into the courtyard. The lead police vehicle was within fifty feet of the courtyard. Flames were engulfing the entire main house. Raven turned the vehicle sharply to the left and shot between and old shed and a barn heading toward the rear of the farm. As he did so, he heard sirens behind him and a loudspeaker commanding him to stop. Ignoring the commands, Raven began driving across the back pasture, veering from side to side to avoid rocks and bushes. Behind him, three police vehicles gave chase, bouncing across the pasture. Raven glanced over his shoulder and saw the squad cars bouncing along behind him. Seeing a rocky hill to his right, he angled toward the left-rear corner of the estate. At times, the vehicle bounced so violently that his head hit the roof. Behind, the police vehicles were faring even worse, bouncing crazily. The fire truck had reached the main house, and firefighters hurried to free their hoses, preparing to fight the fire as clouds of black smoke and flames rose from the house.

As Raven neared the cyclone fence, he glanced at the controls of the snowplow. Familiar with the equipment, he raised the plow and turned directly toward the center of a panel of the fence, gunning the engine. As the plow hit the fence, it held for a moment. Raven's heart sank. The rear wheels began to spin. Then, slowly, the fence began to give, and the vehicle surged forward. The fence snapped apart at a seam, and the vehicle shot forward again. The rocky knoll where he had earlier surveyed the farm appeared before him, and he veered to the left, crashing through small tag alders and willows as he moved away from the pasture. As Raven moved away, the first police vehicle reached the cyclone fence and stopped. Then the driver began to attempt following Raven. Within thirty yards, it became so rough and rocky that it was impossible to give chase in a squad car. The driver pulled the vehicle to a halt. As the officers stepped out of the squad car, they could hear the roaring of the Jeep's engine as Raven crashed deeper and deeper into the woods. By now, he had opened a lead of about two hundred yards on his pursuers.

The terrain kept getting rougher. From his earlier survey, he knew it was only a matter of seconds before he reached heavy timber. Slamming on the brakes, he opened the door, grabbed his weapon and pouch, and jumped from the vehicle, leaving the motor running. He heard the shouts of the officers on the other side of a ridge he'd crossed just moments earlier.

Raven searched feverishly for an escape route that would provide the best cover. To his right, he saw a hill cut by a dark ravine. Ahead of him, the land rose gently up a bushy slope, running into the grove of pines he'd scouted out and climbed the previous day. To his left, the terrain dropped away to a stand of thick alder that flanked the brook and eventually ran down to the highway and his car. Raven made a snap decision and dashed for the dense alders along the brook. Within seconds, he had faded into the brush.

Once in the alders, his woodsman's instincts began to take over, and he ceased running. Crouching in the shadows of a blown-down poplar, he paused, listening for his pursuers. A few moments later, he heard the voices of four police officers as they topped the rise. As they spotted the Jeep, they drew their service revolvers, crouched, and began approaching the vehicle. Raven seized the opportunity to melt farther into the woods, traveling at an angle away from the path of the Jeep and the converging officers. After about fifty yards, he reached the brook. Pausing again, he debated if he should return to his car or head farther into the forest. If he could reach the car undetected, he might make a clean, swift escape. On the other hand, it was unlikely the road was unwatched, and there was a strong possibility that police had already found his vehicle.

He made another snap decision. He would rely on his woodsmanship rather than run the risk of returning to the car. Reckoning that a search party would soon be formed, complete with tracking dogs, Raven waded out into the stream. The icy water topped his boots. Slinging the rifle over his back and carrying the shotgun in his left hand, he waded nearly across. Then reaching shallows near the far bank, he turned right and began wading upstream as swiftly as he could, taking care not to make much noise. Off to his right, he heard the shouts of his pursuers as they fanned out into the woods parallel and ahead of him, about one hundred yards away. Raven moved upstream, trying to recall how far ahead the first tributaries lay. As he rounded the second bend in the stream, he felt a surge of relief as he spotted the first tributary quartering into the stream from the left. Entering the smaller brook, he noted its brownish water, giving evidence of a peat bog ahead and, hopefully, heavy timber. As he rounded a bend, he spotted a small beaver pond framed by the beginning of a dense cedar swamp. As he climbed over the beaver dam, the water rose to his thighs, and his boots encountered mucky bottom. Pleased with the rougher terrain, he waded slowly across the pond, ducking low beneath the branches of the cedars as he entered the swamp.

35

I T WAS GOING TO BE A STEAMY DAY in Manhattan. As Flash
parked his car beside the Federal Office Building, the
smell of car exhaust and hot pavement was beginning to
overtake the city. He entered the building and began climb-
ing the steps toward the office. He was met by a terrifically
excited Henry Grogan.

"Flash, all hell's breaking loose up at the Cerrillo place in
Connecticut. From what we understand, there's a minor war
going up there. As I speak, they're still trying to put out a fire
at the main house. Want to head up there?"

"Hell, yes. Let's go. Run up and let the rest of them know
where we're going. I'll bring the car around," replied Flash,
turning in the midst of the stairs and lumbering back out of
the building. *Hot damn, I knew something was going down.
Nothing like a day in the country*, he thought cheerfully.

Flash drove the car out of the parking lot and up to the
main entrance of the building, where he picked up Grogan.

"What do you know so far?"

"From our reports, we've got three dead Cerrillo soldiers
and two dead dogs," replied Grogan. "In addition, we've got

one captured girlfriend and a roaring fire at the main house. We think the woman is Dom Cerrillo's latest flame, but she ain't talkin'. We have reason to believe Cerrillo and at least one bodyguard were caught in the fire. And there's at least one attacker loose in the woods behind the estate. Any guesses as to who he might be?"

Flash glanced at his partner. "You're not going to like it when I tell you this, Henry, but guess what I had this morning?" he asked, a rueful grin spreading across his face.

"Let me guess. . . . Oh no. No! Could it be, Flash, that you had one of your famous hunches?"

"Right on, Henry. You may not believe it, but as I was getting dressed this morning, I had a funny feeling about our vigilante. What do you think of that?"

"Uncanny. Simply uncanny," mused Grogan, only half joking. "Whoever the hitter is, he must be good. From what I've learned so far, we have two killed by strangulation with a wire, one by rifle, and one by shotgun. So, we either have a small gang of hit men or one hell of a weapons man on our hands." Keeping in touch with headquarters as they drove toward the Cerrillo estate, Flash and Henry continued to speculate about all the possible scenarios of the recent attack.

36

Edging into the cedar swamp, Raven encountered familiar smells and sights that belied the strangeness of the situation. Cedar swamps, sanctuaries from harshness of ordinary light and noise, are similar throughout North America. A few rays of sunshine filtered through the thick branches, and beneath the heavy canopy, Raven made out a few tussocks of green grass. As far as he could see were fallen logs, small pools of water, and above all, the forest floor of layers of dead and decaying needles.

Kneeling, he took stock of his equipment. In the pouch, he had four granola bars and a canteen of water. He still carried the .270 Winchester on its sling across his back and the sawed-off shotgun. On his belt, he had the Finnish knife. In addition, he carried the lighter in his pocket along with the cash in his billfold. His hand stung and throbbed from the Doberman bite. His briefcase, toolbox, and suit carrier were back at the car along with the slacks, loafers, sport coat, and shirt he had been wearing as he traveled. He wondered how much evidence they would provide the authorities. *No time to worry about it now*, he thought.

Crouching low beneath the branches of the cedars, he

angled away from the direction he believed his immediate pursuers were taking. *Soon they'll surround the area and bring in dogs and planes*, he reasoned. *Got to keep moving. Got to stay sharp!*

After traveling through the cedars for approximately half a mile, he found the ground rising slightly. Soon the cedars began to thin out, giving away to a dense grove of poplar interspersed with small pines. Raven saw a small ridge of mixed poplar and hardwoods about one hundred yards ahead. He had to make a decision to stay in the dense cover of the cedars or keep moving. He elected to keep moving, searching for water to hide his scent from tracking dogs. As he edged into the poplars, he heard a helicopter coming swiftly across the trees. About twenty yards ahead of him, Raven saw a huge, blown-down pine. Diving into the cover afforded by its trunk and the soil entangled in its roots, he lay still, his heart pounding. Within seconds, the helicopter pulled over the cedars, circling along its edge.

Above him, the chopper pilot spoke to his companion. "If he's in those cedars, we'll never spot him from the air. But the main search party seems to be moving about a half mile to our right. Shall we head over there?"

"Yeah, but let's pick up a little altitude. Hang me up about five hundred feet over those pines, and I'll see what I can make out through the binocs," his companion replied.

Below them, not daring to look up, Raven hugged the ground. *If they've got more than one chopper and they begin searching in quadrants, I'll have to stay still until dark*, he thought. Then as the helicopter moved off and upward, he began moving away from its path, angling forward and moving in short, controlled bursts of about fifty yards per move. Between moves, Raven would pause to catch his breath and search the woods around him. As he crossed the rise in the poplar woods, he though he heard the baying of hounds far behind him.

Just off the road that ran past the Cerrillo estate, two sheriff's deputies and two highway patrolmen contemplated the rented car. Perplexed with the situation, they radioed to their superiors for permission to break into the vehicle. Tracing the license plates, the Connecticut State Police reported that it was a rental car out of Kennedy Airport. As they considered what to do about the situation, Henry Grogan and Flash Maruska arrived at the main guard gate. After being briefed on the casualty list and what had happened so far, Flash took responsibility for the rental car, ordering the FBI to take over its contents on the claim that it was official business of the organized crime strike force. Immediately, both County Sheriff Clayton Winslow and Lieutenant Arnie Furillo of the Connecticut State Police began arguing that all evidence in the vehicle was really under their respective jurisdictions.

"Goddamn it, guys, let's try cooperating from the outset for a change, shall we?" stormed Flash. "Let's all break into the goddamn car and inventory its contents together, OK?"

Shamed, Winslow and Furillo nodded their agreement.

When they all arrived at the rental car, Winslow took a pick from his pocket and expertly opened the vehicle. Then, together, they began to inventory the clothing and luggage inside.

By midmorning, in addition to increasing numbers of law-enforcement officers, curiosity seekers had begun to take up positions along the shoulders of the road opposite the Cerrillo property. Hurrying to the scene in a variety of vehicles and airplanes, reporters from newspapers and TV stations as far away as New York, Boston, and New Haven were converging on the scene.

Flash looked askance at Grogan. "Looks like we're in for another goddamn circus, Henry," he muttered.

37

OVING ALONG THE EDGE of the poplar woods on the far side of the ridge, Raven stopped periodically and sighted through the scope of his rifle as far as he was able in all directions, carefully selecting his routes for maximum cover and to avoid unpleasant surprises. He startled grouse and deer as he quietly floated through the woods. Occasionally, he encountered ancient stone fences that marked fields long since overgrown to second-growth timber. Paralleling one such ancient fence, he came within fifty yards of a clearing. Sighting through the woods, he made out an abandoned farmhouse and barn. A drive led off to a road that, if followed for a mile or so, would intersect the road where he'd left his rental car.

Got to avoid roads, he told himself. Moving through the woods behind the farm's back pasture, he speculated over the amount of patrolling taking place. *One thing's certain: the pressure is bound to intensify. Need to find someplace to hole up until nightfall.* Topping a rise behind the second farm, he was pleased to discover another small brook that ran to his left through more poplar woods.

This time, he waded downstream, stopping in some hazel brush about fifty yards from the point where the brook crossed the road. He waited about five minutes. As he'd anticipated, he heard a vehicle approaching. Raven flattened himself against the ground, peering beneath the bushes at the approaching vehicle. Two young highway patrolmen scanned the woods on both sides of the vehicle as it moved slowly along the road. Raven buried his head in leaves and grass, praying he wouldn't be detected. Slowly, the squad car pulled away. He rose to his knees. Waiting another five minutes or so, he heard no sound. Resuming his wading, he came to a culvert running beneath the road, about four feet in diameter. He crawled into it, immersing himself in icy water up to his thighs and then nearly up to his armpits. As he emerged through the far end of the culvert, he stopped again, listening. Hearing no vehicles, he continued downstream, relieved at the prospect of escaping the boundaries of the immediate search area without leaving scent for the tracking dogs.

Raven continued downstream and searched for a place to hide until dark. About a half mile from the road, he opened his pouch and removed his canteen and one of the granola bars. He was very thirsty. "Conserve your clean drinking water," he told himself. Although he wasn't hungry, he forced himself to eat half the granola bar. Resisting the urge to gulp too much water, he limited himself to two swallows. "Better save both food and water."

Suddenly aware that he was talking to himself, he registered the incongruity of his situation. "Here I am, halfway across the continent, waging a war only I know I declared, hiding out like an animal from everybody. I wonder if anyone else would understand. Maybe Angela, if I dared to tell her. But telling her might force her to make choices she doesn't want to face. This is a hell of a time to sit around speculating to yourself, Mr. Ravendal." Then, realizing the futility of conducting a one-sided conversation, he surveyed his surroundings again and moved off downstream.

Raven noticed that the terrain generally rose as he moved north and west. He held to a westerly course, wondering how long it would take before he encountered a sizable river or lake, either of which would limit his progress. He knew there were several sizable rivers in the vicinity that ran east and south, eventually entering Long Island Sound many miles downstream. He wished he'd included a map in his pouch.

By early afternoon, he no longer heard the sounds of a search around him. He continued to move in short intervals, pausing wherever cover was thick. From time to time, he heard helicopters and the drone of small planes flying overhead. *I've been lucky so far*, he thought. *It's time to find someplace to hole up.*

After about another mile, he encountered a small brook that ran down a hillside into the stream he'd been following. Turning right, he followed the brooklet uphill. Eventually, he arrived at its source, a small pool fed by a spring bubbling out of a hillside. Glancing about, he realized he was in an abandoned orchard. At the edge of the orchard, he made out the ancient stone foundation of a homestead, abandoned for many years.

Searching behind the foundation, he found what he was looking for: an abandoned root cellar completely overgrown with bittersweet vines and blackberry bushes. Worming his way beneath the thorny branches, he entered the root cellar, where he stashed his weapons and pouch. Then, returning to the spring, he tasted the water. Finding it sweet, he emptied his canteen, refilled it, and drank deeply. He carefully cleaned the dog bite on his hand. Then he took a branch and, backing slowly, carefully brushed out any track he'd left until he reached the root cellar. It was midafternoon.

Crawling into the cellar, he closed his eyes. He began slowly recalling every detail of his home farm, willing himself to sleep. After about ten minutes, his eyelids grew heavy from the fatigue brought on by the stress of the attack and escape, and he slept deeply.

38

GROGAN, MARUSKA, WINSLOW, AND FURILLO surveyed the contents of the rented car.

"Flash, what do you make of this toolbox?" asked Grogan.

"Not much, unless it's got prints on it. It looks like a standard Black & Decker tool chest to me."

"Did you ever see such a floppy top on a first-rate garment bag?" Furillo asked.

Flash looked at the garment bag. "It looks like the top was designed for some kind of a frame that's been removed. Any possibility of tracing it?"

"Christ, I've got one just like it," Furillo claimed. "About two years ago, my credit card company offered a special on these bags. Now, it seems like every time I take a trip, three bags just like it come down the carousel at the airport. I doubt we're going to be able to trace the bag any more than the toolbox. How about the clothes?"

"You ever hear of a Dayton's store?" asked Grogan.

"Well, you wouldn't have," Flash needled. "I mean, when was the last time you bought any new clothes, 1955?"

"Ah, come on, Flash. What about this Dayton's?"

"There are Dayton's stores in a number of midwestern cities, I believe," replied Furillo. "I think the company is now called Dayton-Hudson, with headquarters in both Minneapolis and Detroit. What does the label say?"

"It just says Dayton's," replied Grogan.

"Well, then," Flash interjected, "it looks like we've got a clue. Whoever rented this probably either lives in the Twin Cities or Detroit, near the Twin Cities or Detroit, or once bought a sport coat from one of the Dayton's stores for some reason. Big deal!" Flash turned to Furillo. "Have you got a fix on who rented the car yet?"

"It should be coming through any minute. How much do you want to bet it's been rented in a phony name?"

"Yeah, I know," replied Flash. "But the location of the ID might give us a foothold."

A half hour later, they received word that the driver's license used to rent the car was one reported stolen in California.

Flash groaned. "Well, that really narrows it down. Now we know we have to watch out for someone who once bought a sport coat in or near Minnesota or Michigan at some time in his life and stole an ID in California fairly recently. Whoopee! What size is the jacket, anyhow? At least that might give us a clue about his build."

Furillo tried on the sport coat, smiling as it drooped over his shoulders. "Well, fellows, I'm six feet tall, 175 pounds, and I wear a size forty-two. It looks like the dude who wore this could play middle linebacker for the Giants. This thing is about a forty-six long."

"Now that might help us, someday," stated Flash. "Anything else we ought to note?"

The four officers busied themselves searching the car minutely, looking for anything that might provide clues about the identity or location of the man they were pursuing.

"Don't handle this clothing anymore than you have to," Flash instructed. "I want the lab to go over it—and the car—to see if we can get any hairs or other identification."

"Why the hell didn't you tell me that before I put on the coat?" Furillo laughed. "Now I'm probably gonna be a suspect!"

All four officers burst out laughing and then resumed their search.

39

RAVEN AWOKE IN THE EARLY EVENING to the glow of a spectacular sunset. Slowly, he began flexing his cramped muscles. He was hungry, and the wound from the dog bite on his left hand was throbbing. Searching the area, he found a cache of hazelnuts the squirrels had forgotten the preceding winter. He cracked and ate a few nuts and then slowly ate one of the granola bars, washing it down with springwater from the canteen.

His hunger satisfied, he searched about for some dry twigs, which he brought back to the root cellar. He knew that the branches from the bushes above the root cellar would filter the smoke thrown by a small fire of dry wood. He built a fire and heated the blade of his knife. Then he carefully cleaned the twin punctures from the dog bite with the sterile blade. He didn't attempt a full cauterization but simply cleaned the wounds carefully so that a small bit of blood flowed out. Turning to the back of the root cellar, he found several handfuls of cobwebs, which he pressed into the wounds to coagulate the blood. Once the blood ceased flowing, Raven was satisfied he'd done all he could to prevent infection. As the sun sank below the horizon, he decided it was time to move out.

After heading in a westerly direction for about a mile, he came to a narrow asphalt road. Turning north, he paralleled the highway. Staying back in the brush about fifty yards from the road, he dropped to the ground whenever cars passed. Occasionally, he encountered small farmsteads, which he avoided by moving away from them or crossing the highway. After moving several miles in this fashion, he saw the lights of a country tavern. A number of cars and pickups, as well as four motorcycles, were parked outside.

Raven slowly approached the vehicles and was disappointed to see that none had ignition keys. "By now, I suppose they're talking about the search on TV and radio," he said to himself. "Better stay hidden." Lurking in the brush at the edge of the clearing, he watched the comings and goings of several bar patrons. At about ten o'clock, a burly figure in motorcycle leathers came out, started his motorcycle, and peeled away along the road, passing within ten yards of Raven. After about fifteen minutes, two more bikers emerged, started their cycles, and followed in the direction of the first.

More pickups and cars arrived, and as their occupants entered the bar, Raven could hear the jukebox blaring. Finally, about eleven o'clock, the last biker lurched out of the bar. Carrying a gut full of beer, he reeled slightly as he straddled his motorcycle and fired the engine. Raven moved to the edge of the road. While he waited, he broke down the .270.

Leaving the chopped shotgun in its pouch beside the road, he grasped the barrel of the .270 in his right hand. As the biker neared him, he lunged into the road, swinging the barrel. He smacked the biker square on the forehead, instantly knocking him unconscious. The motorcycle continued on for about twenty feet and then veered into the ditch. Raven ran quickly over to it and shut off its lights and engine.

Returning to the fallen rider, he checked his condition. Noting that the man was still breathing, with a large welt rising across his forehead, Raven muttered to himself, "The Lord looks after drunks and little children." Dragging the biker into the woods, he sat him beside a tree, pulled off his belt, and tied him, hands behind him, around the tree. Quickly fetching his pouch and weapons, he returned to the motorcycle, opened its panniers, and shoved his belongings inside. In a moment of inspiration, he raced back to the fallen motorcyclist, removed his motorcycle cap, and placed it on his head. Then he started the bike, made a U-turn, and headed down the highway in the opposite direction taken by the first three bikers.

A feeling of exhilaration swept over him as he cruised away. *You're not out of the woods yet, Gunar,* he thought. *Better keep watch for patrol cars and stay off the main roads.* Continuing west, he crossed the state line into New York. He followed state highways, passing through the small cities north of New York City and crossing the Hudson just west of Peekskill. From there, he moved into New Jersey, arcing down Highway 202 to Newark.

On the outskirts of Newark, he pulled into the parking lot of a huge discount store. He shopped for a complete change of clothing, another tool kit, and a cheap suitcase. His heart sped up as he approached the cash register. He selected a young clerk. He paid for his purchases in cash, averting his eyes to avoid contact. As he left the cash register, he passed the security guard. When he returned to the motorcycle, he spotted several teenagers standing by it.

"Nice bike, man." The largest of the group smirked. "From Connecticut, huh?"

Not wishing an incident, Raven simply stared into the eyes of the young tough. It worked. Dropping his eyes, the young man muttered, "Come on, let's get out of here, guys. This guy ain't friendly."

Relieved, Raven started the engine. Carrying his purchases under one arm, he pulled out of the parking lot and drove to a fast-food restaurant. He went inside and walked immediately to the restroom. Entering a stall, he quickly changed clothes and went back out to the motorcycle. He slowly cruised the area until he found an unwatched Dumpster, where he dropped the clothes he'd been wearing. Pulling onto a side street, he placed his weaponry into his new tool kit, which he set in the bottom of his pouch. Then he parked the motorcycle on a side street and walked to a populated area.

About twenty minutes later, he hailed a cab to the Newark airport. He bought a one-way ticket in the name of James Wilson on PEOPLExpress to Minneapolis. After he checked his luggage, nearly overcome by fatigue, he headed for an airport snack bar, where he ate his first warm food in forty-eight hours. On the plane an hour later, drained of all emotion, Raven fell into a deep sleep. He didn't awaken until the plane began its descent into Wold-Chamberlain Field in Minneapolis–St. Paul some four hours later.

He was still exhausted after his short flight to Grand Forks. He thought of calling Angela and then decided he needed more rest. Driving back to the farm, he kept dozing off. He opened the windows and slapped himself in the face periodically to stay awake. Finally, totally exhausted, the warrior stepped out of his Ramcharger at his home farmyard. Too exhausted to feed or even greet the horses, he staggered into the house, shedding his clothing as he crossed the bedroom floor. Raven Ravendal finally tumbled into his own bed. He fell into a heavy, dark slumber marred by fitful wakenings and nightmares of being pursued by a slavering pack of wolves.

40

September 1977

KILLINGS OF MAFIA FIGURES around the country increased tenfold. As they walked away from a boxing match in Las Vegas, two Mafia enforcers were slain by a man wearing heavy makeup. The assailant sped away with another man in a waiting car. And in Los Angeles, Nate Gottlieb died instantly when a slug from a .30-06 deer rifle—fired from one hundred yards away—pierced his chest as he walked from the bank to his automobile.

The big news, though, was the raid on the Cerrillo estate. As word of the raid and manhunt spread across the nation, all branches of the media arrived on the scene, clamoring for photographs and interviews. Several scuffles between reporters and sheriff's deputies ensued. The cover of the country's most famous weekly newsmagazine carried a photo of the burned Cerrillo house under the headline OPEN SEASON ON THE MAFIA?

When the bound biker was discovered the following day, yelling to be released from the tree where Raven had tied him, hordes of reporters arrived on the scene, along with sheriff's deputies, FBI agents, and state patrol officers. Again, scuffles erupted as reporters attempted to photograph and interview the fallen biker with the huge purple goose egg on his forehead. His blackened eyes resembled a raccoon's. Immediately, a search was instituted at all levels for the missing motorcycle, complete with an all-points bulletin for its unknown rider.

At the Cerrillo estate, teams of experts combed the grounds to search for clues. Speculation was rampant as to the number of attackers. Back at FBI headquarters in New York, a jurisdictional dispute among various law-enforcement agencies raged over who had the right to interview Dom Cerrillo's blonde companion.

Within hours, a Cerrillo attorney was dispatched to counsel her. Having been advised of her constitutional rights, she ceased cooperating with police after one overzealous investigator told her she could be held as a suspected accomplice to whoever had attacked the estate. Shortly thereafter, aware of her instant celebrity status and the possibility of becoming wealthy, the blonde made two telephone calls unbeknownst to her Cerrillo attorney—one to a private lawyer, the second to a literary agent. It was another chapter in what one humorist had already dubbed "The Year of the Bimbo."

Within days, as the last person to see Dom Cerrillo alive and the only person known to have spoken to the Dashing Vigilante (as the media had named the attacker), young Darla Van Ende was besieged by offers to appear on talk shows, give interviews to the major networks, and sell movie and publishing rights to her story. The temptation to embellish the facts proved too much for her; soon she deliberately leaked just enough false information about the Dashing Vigilante (whom she'd actually never clearly seen in her panicked flight amid the smoke and gunfire) to tantalize all those clamoring for her attention. The most lurid headlines and stories were run by the trashy tabloids found at supermarket checkout counters.

As the entire continent became caught up in stories about Darla's contributions and the magazine cover story, hits on Mafia figures increased geometrically. Branches of the underworld, from drug smugglers in Florida to drug dealers across the nation, began to panic. Some went underground. Some seized the opportunity to eliminate their competition. And some attacked their enemies in the mistaken belief that their enemies, rather than freelance vigilantes, had hit them.

Two teams of tracking dogs were brought in to follow Raven's tracks away from the Cerrillo compound. One team became completely confused by the tracks of an ambitious freelance photographer who had attempted to creep up on the Cerrillo estate from the woods behind it, equipped with a powerful telephoto lens. When he saw the dogs coming in his direction, he panicked and led the officers and hounds on a frantic chase before he was found, scratched and exhausted, two miles behind the estate. The other team followed Raven's tracks to the first creek but then lost his scent. Hours later, entering the cedar swamp, they picked up his scent again and then lost it. The result was an intense aerial and foot-by-foot search of the dense cedar swamp. The search was marred considerably by the fact that most of the members of the search party were completely unaccustomed to working such dense thickets and kept getting lost. Finally, furious and exasperated, the dog handlers called in their bloodhounds and refused to continue the search.

Flash Maruska and Henry Grogan, having completed their search of the rental car, contemplated the circus taking shape around them.

"Well, Flash, I do believe it's going to be impossible to do any more meaningful police work around here. What do you think?"

"Yeah, I agree. We might as well head back to the office and try to piece together what we know so far. With all the killing going on, my charts are becoming hopelessly obsolete. And I miss Rosalee's cooking. Want to come over for dinner tomorrow night?"

"I'd love to. Are you off your diet?"

"Until Rosalee weighs me in."

On the way back to New York, Grogan questioned Flash, "What do you make of it, big guy? I mean, do you think the raid was the work of one man, acting alone?"

"I'm not sure. If it is only one person, he's gotta be one hell of a man."

The two friends drove on in silence, each lost in images from the Cerrillo massacre: the garrote lying beside the fallen guard, the two dead Dobermans, the dead guards, and the charred corpses found in the ruins of the burned house.

Flash's last image was of the two chimneys at each end of the house, all that was left standing, looming against the sky, as he and Henry drove away from the estate.

"I don't think I'd want to go up against him armed, in the woods," Grogan offered, unable to endure silence for too long.

"What?" snapped Flash, startled out of his daydream.

"I don't think I'd want to take on this vigilante if he was armed and in the woods. Would you?"

Flash pondered the question a moment and then responded, "Not on his terms, on his turf. I think our man, assuming it's only one man, would be damned formidable." Then, after several minutes of additional reflection, he added, "Almost superhuman."

41

RAVEN'S HAND CONTINUED TO THROB where the Doberman's teeth had raked it. Although it had begun to scab over, the back of the hand was swollen, and there were angry red streaks running away from the lacerations left by the teeth. Raven debated the wisdom of seeking medical attention as he continued treating himself for several days with poultices and other home remedies. Although the infection didn't appear to be spreading, it didn't improve either. On the fourth day after he returned home, the telephone rang.

"I've missed you," he heard Angela say.

"I've missed you, too."

"What does a girl need to do to get an invitation to come out and go horseback riding? Lose all her pride and ask, or wait until she becomes an old maid?"

"I haven't been feeling well. I got bit on the hand, and it seems it's become infected."

"Have you seen a doctor?"

"No. I didn't think I'd need one."

"I'd like to come and nurse you back to health," she said, trying to keep things light.

A feeling of relief swept over Raven. "I think that may be the best medicine I could take."

"I'll be there Friday evening. And I don't have any classes until Tuesday noon. So I'll have plenty of time for nursing."

"I'd like that. I'll go see the doctor before you come and see what advice he can offer. I'm sure he'll prescribe some of the Chianti you brought last time, so you'd better get two more bottles to go with your linguine."

"It's a deal! I'll hurry out as soon as I finish my last class Friday. I missed you."

"It'll be great to see you again. And the Appaloosa misses you, too." Immediately, his thought turned to Kari and then to the scene at the Cerrillo estate. Raven wondered if Angela would guess what he'd done and how he'd handle things if she did.

Back in Manhattan, it was a gray day marked by a steady, chilling drizzle. Flash Maruska sat in Lieutenant Massey's office, rain dripping off his trench coat. "Massey, I'd like to talk to you some more about those folks who came to see you—from Wisconsin or Michigan or wherever the hell it was—about that dead hooker last fall. Could you tell me about what size they were?"

"They were both big guys—about six two, 220 or so. Why are you so curious about them?"

"I don't know. A few of the clues we've got about the raid on the Cerrillo estate point to the Midwest, that's all."

Massey smiled. "Well, if it's any consolation, it seems as though great minds run in the same channels. I already did a little checking to find out whether or not the father of the young hooker owned a Ruger .22."

"How did you go about that, Massey?"

Massey smiled sheepishly. "Maybe I wasn't too subtle about it. It seemed like a shot in the dark at the time. I guess it sounds pretty stupid now, but I called her father and asked if anybody in the family owned a 10/22 Ruger. He denied it."

Flash rolled his eyes. "Brilliant. Anything else? Any follow-up?"

"Nope. Like I say, it seemed unlikely. You got anything that makes it look like anything less than a long shot?" Massey's shrewd eyes narrowed.

"Not a hell of a lot. Except that whoever made the raid up in Connecticut had to be one hell of a woodsman. Not much ties in. Just for the hell of it, give me their names and addresses, will you? I may get around to following up on them sometime," Flash added casually.

Massey arched his eyebrows and then turned to the file cabinet behind him and pulled out a file labeled *Ravendal, Kari* from his file of unsolved homicides. He found the address of her next of kin, wrote it on a piece of paper, and shoved it at Flash. "If anything big comes of it, Flash, I could use a little recognition, OK?"

"Never let it be said that Flash Maruska fails to give credit where credit is due." As he unfolded his massive frame from the chair, a few drops of water from his raincoat splattered the papers on Massey's desk. "Sorry." Flash grinned. "See you around!"

"Yeah, see you around. Good hunting," he added as he watched the big man step out of his office and move down the corridor. *There goes a helluva cop*, he thought.

The day before Angela arrived, Raven finally went into town and saw a doctor. He told his aging general practitioner he'd been bitten by a coyote he'd thought was shot dead before he walked up on it. When asked if he wanted a rabies shot, Raven declined, but he did obtain a tetanus shot and a massive dosage of antibiotic pills. By the time Angela arrived the next day, the hand looked a lot better. They spent Saturday and Sunday idyllically—cooking, riding in the woods, and making love. As they sat looking into the fire on Sunday night, Raven finally decided to talk to Angela about the Cerrillo raid.

"I suppose you've read what happened to Dom Cerrillo. How do you feel about it?"

Gazing intently into the fire, Angela's eyes darkened. "Good. It's good. How do you feel?"

Raven sat silently for a long time, watching the flames. Finally, choosing his words carefully, he offered, "It was something that needed doing, if there's any justice in the world, on account of Kari and your father."

After another long silence, Angela, still looking into the flames, reached over and began running her fingers through Raven's hair. Then suddenly, she moved, kneeling next to Raven. Gazing deeply into his eyes again, she said, "Don't say anything more. Ever. Just know that if you ever need me, I'll do all I can."

Pulling her to him, Raven buried his face in her breast, holding her tightly. As waves of emotion swept over them, they made love before the crackling flames, knit more closely than ever before.

42

T DAWN, AS ANGELA LAY SLEEPING, Raven headed
out to his smithy next to the stable and fired up
the forge. Slipping quietly back into the house, he
found his sawed-off shotgun, the Ruger 10/22, and the .270,
together with the stock assembly and the hollowed-out camera. Using his bellows, he soon had the coals in a white-
hot heat. As he worked, Honey and Money, the two ravens
he and Kari had raised from chicks, flew over the building,
croaking a welcome and farewell on their way to the edge
of the grove.

Using his tongs, Raven set all the weapons into the coals.
The flames flared high when the wood from the stock and
pump of the shotgun and the plastic of the camera and razor
ignited. After a few minutes, the plastic and wood were completely consumed by the flames. Then, taking his tongs and
his hammer, Raven began beating the barrels flat, quenching
and firing them, again and again, shaping them first into bars;
then, finally, into blades. Intent on his work, he failed to see
the rented automobile pulling into his driveway and heading
toward the smithy.

Finally, hearing a croak, he looked up and saw Honey and Money had returned. He noticed the sound of a car motor, and he looked up as it pulled into the farmyard. The door opened, and the huge figure of Flash Maruska emerged and walked up to Raven.

"Are you one of the Ravendals?"

"Yes. I'm Gunar. Which one of us are you looking for?"

"Actually, I'm looking for both of you. Does your brother, Lorne, live here, too?"

"He lives over on the other side of that grove. What can I do for you?" he asked, already sensing that Flash was some type of a policeman. Both men sized each other up. Each intuited the physical strength—as well as the strength of character—of the other.

Dropping his gaze to Raven's work, Flash asked, "What are you doing?"

"Shaping some pieces of steel into something useful. I think I'll probably make these pieces of bar steel into plowshares for my little garden tractor over there. But I haven't really decided exactly what I'll do with them yet. We Norwegians hate to waste anything that can be useful, you know."

"An admirable trait." Flash paused. "You asked if you could help me. I ought to tell you who I am. My name is Maruska. I'm with the US Department of Justice's organized crime strike force. I got your name and your brother's from Lieutenant Massey of the NYPD. I'd like to talk to you about an investigation."

"Do you mind if I ask you some questions as well?"

"No, not at all. Fire away."

Raven took a deep breath and looked directly into Maruska's eyes. "I'm wondering why you're investigating something so far from New York. And, if you're investigating organized crime, I'm wondering if you've caught the animal that killed my niece." Then, turning from Flash, he pointed out to the corral. "See that little Appaloosa over there? That was Kari's mare. We raised it together, from a filly to a champion. Do you have any daughters, Mr. Maruska?"

Taken off guard, Flash looked again at Raven. The questioning wasn't following the usual pattern. "Normally, I ask the questions," he replied. "But to answer yours, no, we haven't come up with any leads on who strangled your niece. And my wife and I have no children."

The men stood looking at one another for a time.

Then Raven broke the silence. "I understand you have a hard time catching killers within the ranks of the Mafia. Is that true? I mean—do you actually catch their hit men?"

Flash looked into Raven's eyes again and then let his eyes drop. He glanced again at the Appaloosa. "What you say is true. We don't often make a collar on Mafia hit men. And, as you know, we strongly suspect the Cerrillo family was involved in your niece's death. But we don't have any proof. To be honest, I doubt we'll ever solve the crime. From what we know, based strictly on rumors from informers on the street, both of the men who ordered the killing are dead now. Their names, we believe, were Vito and Dom Cerrillo. Actually, right now, I'm looking into what happened to them. Part of my job is coordinating all activities involving organized crime in the southern district of New York."

Raven pumped the bellows again, keeping the coals white hot. "Excuse me, Mr. Maruska, but I'd like to finish hammering out these blades while I still have the coals nice and hot."

Watching Raven work, Maruska could see the muscles bulging in his forearms and hands. *He's an incredibly powerful man*, he noted. As he watched, he couldn't help but admire how adeptly Raven handled his tools. It was also apparent that, unlike most people Flash had interrogated in the course of his work, Raven showed no fear or apprehension over the questioning. Maruska's instincts told him Raven knew something about the recent Mafia violence, but his utter lack of fear over being questioned took him somewhat aback. Ordinarily, using his interrogator's skills, he could play upon the uneasiness of the suspect. He'd usually make psychological headway by leveraging that discomfort. Sometimes he'd actually get confessions from nervous suspects who spoke too much for their own good under interrogation. Raven definitely didn't fit the usual profile of a guilty man. *At least he doesn't seem to feel any guilt*, thought Maruska.

After he'd finished quenching the steel, Raven left the bars on the apron of the smithy. Then, before removing his gloves, he held one of his hands aloft and let out a piercing whistle. Immediately, one of the ravens flapped off the roof of the stable and landed on Raven's fist. "Say hello to the nice man, Honey," he commanded. The raven cocked his head to one side and croaked a guttural noise that sounded like *hello*.

Amazed, Maruska exclaimed, "Why, hello back to you! Can both of those ravens talk?"

"Just a few words. They were our pets, Kari's and mine. She's the one who kept working to teach them words when they were young. After we released them back into the wild, they decided to hang around the place. So now they're sort of half-tame and half-wild. But they like to come around for handouts, and they sort of act like a warning system, letting me know when I have visitors. I doubt I would've noticed you driving up today if they hadn't flown back and announced you."

"I'm truly sorry about your niece," Flash offered. *Revenge*, he thought, *nearly as powerful a motivator as fear or greed.*

"What brings you all the way out here, Mr. Maruska? From what I've been reading lately, Mafia wars are going on all over the country. Surely there isn't any Mafia activity way up here in northern Minnesota?"

Flash caught the ironic note in Raven's voice. "No, northern Minnesota and the Dakotas appear to be free of organized crime activity. I'm here to ask you and your brother some questions because we think some of the hits may have been made by a person or persons outside the Mafia. So we decided to look into some of the crime victims. Do you mind answering my questions?"

As he spoke, Angela opened the kitchen door and walked up to them. Instantly recognizing her, Flash's mouth dropped open. "Angela Simone!" he exclaimed. "What brings you way out here? The last I heard, you quit prosecuting and were teaching law at NYU!"

"I'm on leave from NYU. I thought I'd get as far as possible from the New York rat race, so I took a visiting professorship at the University of North Dakota. We met in the law library," she said, smiling as she walked over to Raven and slipped her hand around his waist. "What brings you way out here?"

"Trying to tie together a few loose ends in our endless war against organized crime." He shrugged. "I was just asking Mr. Ravendal some questions. But he has more questions for me than I do for him."

A flicker of anger sprang up in Angela's eyes. "You're not likely to find any leads in the battle against organized crime way up here. I'm wondering what brings you to the Ravendals."

Noting the sudden change in the tone of the meeting, Flash decided to push a bit. "You seem pretty defensive. Are you aware of any reason Mr. Ravendal shouldn't answer all my questions?"

"No one has an obligation to answer the questions of a law-enforcement officer until they know why they're being interrogated," she parried. "Do you have a reasonable suspicion that someone here is involved in illegal activity?"

"I'm not sure. But I'm wondering why you're interceding in my questioning. Until you came into the picture, Mr. Ravendal and I were having a perfectly reasonable conversation."

"Well, I don't like your tone. And I know you'd never come all the way up here just to ask general questions—not without a specific purpose. All I'm saying is I want to know why you're here."

"Is Mr. Ravendal your client?"

"Raven is my friend. As a friend, I'd like to know what's going on, so I can give him the benefit of my knowledge. Are you going to tell me why you're here or not?"

"Mr. Maruska," Raven interjected, "my conscience is clear. I'm not afraid to answer your questions, as long as you'll answer mine. So let's start with my first question: Why are you way out here—a place free of organized crime—when you have such a fight on your hands back in New York? I ask that in the general, philosophical sense. If you don't think those evil bastards are operating way up here in northern Minnesota, why are you here? Why aren't you concentrating on organized crime figures in your jurisdiction?"

Maruska flushed with anger at the questions. This interview definitely wasn't going the way he'd planned.

"I've got the right to investigate anything I see fit! We're doing plenty to zero in on the Mafia, you can rest assured about that!"

"Now *you* seem a bit defensive. You're not ashamed to be chasing after the remote possibility that a crime victim might hit back, rather than going after the Mafia itself, are you?"

Maruska flushed again. "I'm not ashamed of a goddamn thing, Mr. Ravendal." Then, turning to his car, he walked to the back door and opened it, secretly pleased with the interchange. Reaching inside, he pulled out the sport coat he had found in Raven's abandoned rental car back in the woods near the Cerrillo estate. "If you've got nothing to worry about, Mr. Ravendal, I don't suppose you'd mind putting on this coat for me, would you?"

Again, Angela interceded. "Mr. Ravendal has no obligation to do anything for you until you explain your specific purpose. And he certainly doesn't need to try on any clothes for you. Raven, you don't have to put on any clothes for Mr. Maruska or answer any of his questions until he tells you his purpose and whether you're under suspected of a crime."

"Are you advising Mr. Ravendal as his lawyer now? Why does someone whose conscience is so clear need to enlist the services of a skilled lawyer?"

Stepping forward, Raven looked directly into Maruska's eyes again. "I don't think I like your tone, Mr. Maruska. And I don't know what authority you have to come onto my place. But I've never turned anyone off my land in my life. I try to practice medieval hospitality here. I tell all my guests they're welcome to anything I have and they can stay as long as they like. And I usually ask them their life's story and invite them in for some food or coffee. The two of you are acting like a couple of New Yorkers. But I don't see any reason why you shouldn't state exactly what your business is so I can determine whether you're a friend or foe, do you? When you ask me to put on a coat, I guess I ought to know the reason why. Are you trying to trick me into something?"

"Raven, I can assure you he doesn't come with a friendly purpose, no matter how friendly he acts," Angela asserted. "He's here about some crime or other, and you have a right to know what he's investigating. So what is it, Flash?"

Realizing he'd get no further without announcing his purpose, Flash acquiesced. "I'm here investigating the killings at the Cerrillo estate. We found this sport coat in a rented car in the woods near the property. We think it may belong to a person involved in the attack on the estate. Are you willing to put on the coat, Mr. Ravendal?"

"Raven, unless he tells you he has a reasonable suspicion—beyond the fact that the Ravendal family has been victimized by the Mafia—you have no obligation to do anything for him. That sport coat might fit a lot of people."

Raven smiled at Maruska, toying with him. "Mr. Maruska, what if the sport coat does fit? Will that prove to you that it's mine, or simply that someone my size wore it?"

"Have you ever bought clothes at Dayton's in Minneapolis?" Flash inquired.

"I certainly have. And so has nearly everyone else in Minnesota, North and South Dakota, and western Wisconsin. So if the coat doesn't fit, what will that tell you?"

"I guess it'll tell me that you're not the owner of the sport coat. I don't know where that will take me in my investigation."

"I'm curious what you mean by that," Raven pressed. "I mean, you call yourself the organized crime strike force. How is this visit to the frozen north a strike against organized crime? It doesn't exist here. Is it part of your duties, as a strike force against organized crime, to hunt down private individuals who strike at organized crime themselves? Or are you here to satisfy your own curiosity about something?"

Again, Maruska flushed at Raven's words. "No police force and no organized society can tolerate individuals taking the law into their own hands. Vigilantism might have sometimes been a good thing in the Old West, but in a modern society, when private citizens take up arms against each other, chaos is certain to be the result."

"Are you sure? What modern society has been made chaotic by a private citizen striking against organized, career criminals? I'd think you'd welcome a little chaos within the ranks of the Mafia any way you could get it. Don't you think your priorities are a little mixed up? While you're here, what's going on with the Cerrillo family?"

"We're watching them very closely. We think more heads will roll. Several cousins are jockeying for power. In the meantime, the war between the Cerrillos and the Gambuccis continues—and every day we're hearing about more hits on mafiosi by solo operators all over the county. Now, I've answered your questions. Here's mine again: Are you willing to put on the coat?"

"Mr. Maruska, Mr. Ravendal makes a good point. Your trip out here has little to do with your official duties as part of the organized crime strike force. Why is it that police always seem to resent private organizations assisting them in their work? I'm thinking about all the trouble the Guardian Angels have had getting police to recognize them in cities all over the country."

Flash smiled at her. "I always admire the way a good lawyer can change the subject. Angela, if you don't mind, I believe you're interrupting me. I asked you a question, Mr. Ravendal. Are you going to try on the coat?"

Raven looked at him a moment and then walked over to the corral fence. Immediately, the Appaloosa ran up to him, nuzzling his neck. He stroked the horse's velvety muzzle and then turned to Maruska. "If it doesn't fit, will you head out and let me go about my business? Will you go back to New York and devote your valuable time to catching the scum that actually killed our Kari?"

"You have my promise on that, regardless of whether or not the coat fits."

Raven reached for the coat. Then, silently inhaling as he slid his arms into the coat, he flexed the enormously powerful block of muscle in his shoulders and upper arms. Years of pitching hay bales, sawing and loading pulpwood and timber, and athletic workouts and weight lifting had endowed Raven with incredible shoulder, upper arm, and chest muscles. Raven slowly began to expand and flex them. As he pulled on the sport coat, the seams of the shoulders and armpits began to tear and then suddenly split. Removing the coat, he handed the misshapen and torn garment back to Maruska. "Does that satisfy you?"

Flash looked deeply into Raven's eyes. As he gazed into their gray depths, he felt a shiver run down his spine. Finally, he let his eyes drop. Then he looked again at Raven. "I still think it may be you. But this sport coat isn't of any use as a lead."

"Will you be going back to New York, then? And will you be working hard to get the Cerrillo soldiers who killed Kari?"

"I guess my business is finished here, for now."

Turning without a handshake, he walked back to the car, opened the rear door, and threw the sport coat inside. Slamming the door, he turned again to Raven and Angela. He opened the front door of the car and then paused. "My advice to you, Mr. Ravendal, is to stick to your farming. And pay attention to your lovely friend there."

Raven gave him a grim smile. "Good hunting, Mr. Maruska," he said, raising his right hand in farewell.

Maruska lowered himself into the car and then slowly pulled out of the farmyard. As he drove away, the ravens swooped past his windshield and accompanied him partway down the driveway. At the road, Maruska made a left turn, heading back toward the small town. After about a half mile, he came to the Lorne Ravendal driveway. As he approached the mailbox, he saw a blond teenager raising a plume of dust as he raced his three-wheeled ATV toward the intersection. Suddenly inspired, Flash pulled his car to a halt as the ATV reached the mailbox. Rolling down the window, he shouted, "Is your name Ravendal?"

Shutting off his engine, the boy answered, "Yeah, I'm Lars Ravendal. Are you lost?"

"No, I'm not lost, but I've got a question for you," said Flash. He pulled the car off on the shoulder of the road, got out, and opened the rear door. Removing the torn sport coat, he carried it across the road toward the boy. "Ever see this before?" he asked.

Little Lars looked at the sport coat and then looked up. "It looks like my uncle Raven's. But it's torn. Do you want me to take it to him?"

"No, you've answered my question. Your uncle Raven already tried it on, and it didn't fit him," answered Maruska. "How do you like living on a farm?"

"I love it. I'm going to be a partner one day."

"You've got a beautiful life ahead of you," said Flash, getting back into the car. "Good luck with your farming!" Flash slowly pulled away.

Ten minutes later, Flash drove up to a rural general store and filling station. Walking inside, he found Henry Grogan absently leafing through a farming magazine. Grogan glanced up. "Any leads, Flash? I sure hope coming to the boondocks wasn't a wild-goose chase. I've never been so bored in my life."

"Nothing worth following up on at this time," said Flash, smiling. Then, dropping his huge hand on Grogan's shoulder, he steered Grogan outside to the car. "Let's head back to the Big Apple, Henry. I think we're a little out of our element up here, don't you?"

"Yeah, all this fresh air is starting to make me sick. Let's head back to where we can see what we breathe."

Back at the Ravendal farm, Little Lars sped into Raven's yard on his ATV, slamming on the brakes. "Raven!"

Raven and Angela walked out the kitchen door, their arms around one another's waists. "Whoa! Slow down. What's up, Lars?"

"A big man stopped me out on the road and asked me who I was. After I told him, he got out and showed me a sport coat that looked just like yours. But it was torn. He asked me if I'd ever seen it before."

"What did you tell him?" asked Raven.

"I told him it looked like my uncle Raven's. Then he told me you had already tried it on. Did I do the right thing?"

Smiling at him, Raven answered, "Yeah. The man had a question, and you answered as best you could. Angela just made a fresh blueberry pie with some of those wild Canadian berries. Want some?"

Little Lars's eyes lit up. "You bet!" he answered.

Laughing, the three of them turned and headed back through the kitchen door, into the house.

Flash Maruska stared at the highway ahead as he and Grogan crossed the flat prairies of the Red River Valley on their way to Grand Forks. He hadn't spoken for more than fifty miles. Respecting his friend's silence, Grogan watched the farmsteads as they drove through the richest farmland in the world. Finally, Flash's huge stomach began to rumble. "God, am I hungry. And I hate that goddamn airline food. Want to join Rosalee and me for dinner tonight when we're back in New York?"

"Sure. You know me, the lonesome bachelor. I'd love it! Where shall we go?"

"Little Italy," answered Maruska. "Let's head down to the Little Italy."

ACKNOWLEDGMENTS

This book would never have been written without the support and hard work of the love of my life, Pat. Her ideas, encouragement, proofreading, and typing were invaluable for this novel, much like her day-to-day inspiration to persevere in my career as a trial lawyer.

Also, Barbara Haislet's careful reading, comments, and constructive criticism were most appreciated. Traci Lambrecht's inspiration and support has been a godsend.

I also must thank Jim Westby, former Minneapolis vice and homicide detective, for taking the time to read the manuscript and verify the history of prostitution during the late 1970s, when the Minnesota Pipeline was exposed. Unfortunately, the same practices persist to the present day.

A final word to johns all over the world: prostitution is most assuredly not a victimless crime. Whenever you patronize a prostitute, you are aiding and abetting an evil, loathsome criminal enterprise.

ABOUT THE AUTHOR

J erry Rice is a Harvard educated trial lawyer who has handled and tried a wide variety of cases in courts at all levels throughout the United States since the early 1960s. He is the author of two law-related books and thousands of briefs and memoranda as well as occasional poetry, short stories and memoirs. This is his first novel. He regards himself as a member of our justice system, rather than a businessman. Vindicating the constitutional rights of his clients has given him great satisfaction throughout his career. He is a native of Roseau, Mn., in the far northwest corner of the state and is an avid outdoorsman and conservationist. He and his wife Pat love world travel and the cultural life of the Twin Cities of Minnesota and Taos, New Mexico.